GHOSTS FROM THE PAST

GHOSTS FROM THE PAST

•

Glen Ebisch

AVALON BOOKS
NEW YORK

Published by Thomas Bouregy & Co., Inc.
160 Madison Avenue, New York, NY 10016

Library of Congress Cataloging-in-Publication Data

Ebisch, Glen Albert, 1946–.
  Ghosts from the past / Glen Ebisch.
      p. cm.
  ISBN 978-0-8034-9978-2
1. New England—Fiction.   I. Title.

  PS3605.B57G47 2009
  813'.6—dc22

                                        2009012801

PRINTED IN THE UNITED STATES OF AMERICA
ON ACID-FREE PAPER
BY HADDON CRAFTSMEN, BLOOMSBURG, PENNSYLVANIA

Chapter One

Marcie had felt that she was being watched. She'd
read that some people have a sort of sixth sense that sends
a signal when they're being stared at, even when their
backs are turned. And that was the way she had felt back
at the inn when she dropped off her things and asked the
proprietor for directions to the Hayes farm. She had been
vaguely aware of someone sitting in the lobby and of a
waitress setting tables in the dining room, but Marcie had
been so focused on getting the directions straight that she
hadn't paid attention to her feelings. Now she wished she
had.

Marcie glanced repeatedly into the rearview mirror as
she drove down the road. There was no one behind her,
just a long, empty ribbon of black snaking around the
hillsides of Vermont. Instead of making her feel relieved,
the absence of traffic left her feeling more alone than
ever. This was her first trip by herself for *Roaming New*

England Magazine. In the past she had traveled with Amanda Vickers, her senior editor, but Amanda had to stay behind at the office this time because of staffing changes, so Marcie was on her own. The four-hour drive from the coast of southern Maine to the middle of Vermont, along a mix of highways and local roads, had been lonely and tiring.

Marcie was planning to spend the next five days in Vermont checking out five stories that the magazine had received letters about from local residents. The story she was investigating this afternoon, from a man living on a farm just outside of Doric, Vermont, seemed the least promising. The letter itself had been sketchy at best, and her phone conversation two days ago had produced little more than his repeated comment in a cranky voice that he "wasn't tellin' her any more until he saw her face-to-face." Not a prospect she was looking forward to. His confusing directions had forced her to stop at the inn to confirm that what she had written down from his ramblings would actually get her to the farm.

About three miles out of town, Marcie made a right turn onto Grove Road, spotting the large oak tree that Mrs. Evans, the woman back at the inn, had told her to look for as a landmark. She checked her odometer because the way into the farm was supposed to be about a quarter of a mile from the turn. Just past the quarter-mile point she spotted a gravel lane off to the left. A rotting post that might once have held a sign was the only indication that there was anything to be found in that direction. Marcie turned into the lane, which proved to be so narrow that branches from trees bordering the lane reached out and scraped the sides of the car as she slowly bumped along.

Three-tenths of a mile later, according to the odometer, the lane opened up into a farmyard. A house with a rickety front porch and about half its shutters stood off to the right. About thirty feet to the left was a barn that might once have been painted red, although most of the boards had weathered back to the bare wood. Marcie turned off the engine and listened for a moment.

What she didn't hear surprised her. She had been on a few farms back in the Midwest when her father was stationed there in the military. This close to the main house there was usually something to be heard, at the very least the sound of animals or machinery. Here there was nothing aside from the faint insect buzz of late May. She got out of the car and examined its sides for damage. Most of the marks seemed to be superficial, certainly nothing to worry about on car six years old with a trade-in value that was already laughable. But her car was in pristine condition compared to the old blue pickup truck parked alongside the barn. Rust was eating its way up both fenders, the right rear light was smashed, and the back window of the cab was held together with a crosshatching of duct tape.

Marcie turned quickly when she heard a screen door open behind her with a painful squeal of rusty hinges. It slammed shut with a bang behind a short, thin man. He stood on the porch, hopping from foot to foot as if Marcie was just about the most exciting thing he'd seen in years. Marcie guessed that he didn't get many visitors.

As he came down off the porch in a sort of hobbling

run, she could see that he was old. He was wearing loose, threadbare jeans and a faded blue T-shirt several sizes too large, looking like a scarecrow come to life. When he got closer, Marcie could see that his eyes were bloodshot, and the salt-and-pepper stubble on his face hadn't seen a razor in days. The sides of his mouth were sunken in where he was clearly missing a number of teeth. He gave her an anxious smile and moved his arms all sorts of ways before finally extending his right hand. His nervous energy reminded Marcie of friends of her father who had a problem with the bottle and tried to hide their lack of focus with all kinds of pointless action.

"Hi there. You must be the girl from the magazine. I'm Seldon Hayes. Everybody calls me Sel."

"Marcie Ducasse," she replied, shaking his damp hand and then resisting the urge to wipe hers on her slacks.

He looked her up and down with a frank stare that was unnerving. But then his eyes drifted away, and he seemed to have forgotten why she was there.

"So is that the famous barn?" Marcie asked, looking across the deserted yard and trying to get him back on track.

His eyes regained focus, and he grinned happily. "That's it," he announced with a note of feverish pride in his voice. "That is *the* place."

He studied the barn as if seeing if for the first time himself. Then his stare came back to her.

"Are you sure that you're old enough for this job?"

From some men Marcie would have taken that as an insult and replied acerbically. But Sel was such a weird character that she decided to be more charitable—and more cautious.

"I think I can handle it," she said with a smile.

Sel nodded and did a quick shuffle in place as if he could hardly contain some secret happiness.

"I hope you can. I hope you can," he said, nodding like a puppet. Then he strutted across the yard toward the barn without a backward glance, as if he assumed his enthusiasm was contagious enough to draw Marcie along.

When he got to the barn, he began pulling on one of the closed double doors. It was hanging partially off its hinges and rubbed on the ground. A deep rut showed that this was his normal way of doing things. Marcie thought about offering to help but doubted that he would appreciate it. He grunted and pulled, cursing in a genial sort of way, making the whole thing seem like a daily ritual. Finally he managed to get the door about halfway open.

"Come on inside, missy," he said, turning to Marcie and nodding happily. Then he disappeared into the darkness.

Giving the bright spring sun a last look, Marcie followed him into the barn. She saw nothing at first but shadows; then her eyes began to adjust, helped by the shafts of light filtering between the boards that made up the barn's walls. What she noticed next was the smell. A stunning mix of mildew, old hay, ancient manure, and something stronger, perhaps the decaying body of some animal that had sought out the barn as a final resting place.

Pincerlike fingers came out of the shadows and fastened around her lower arm. Marcie suppressed a yelp of surprise.

"You have to come all the way inside to see it," Sel said, pulling her along.

Marcie stumbled several times before her eyes adjusted enough to see what was in front of her, which seemed to be broken bales of hay and a scattering of pieces of farm equipment that she couldn't identify. She hated being dragged about and was ready to wrench herself free from Sel, when he stopped and released her arm as suddenly as he had grabbed it.

"There it is," he said, pointing toward the ceiling.

Marcie looked up. There was the outline of a hayloft, and above it soared the peak of the barn. It seemed so much higher from the inside than it had from the farmyard that she felt for a moment as if she were standing in a rustic cathedral. There was a fluttering and a flash of white as some bird made a quick trip from one side to the other. Seeing a sign of life made her feel better.

"What am I looking for, Sel?"

He snorted at her ignorance and pointed a trembling finger. "That beam right there, girl, the one at the front end of the hayloft. The ropes were looped right over it and tied. That's where we found all three of them hanging."

Sel walked over and stood right under the beam, staring up at it as if mesmerized.

"This is the spot—the devil's spot."

Marcie saw a wide beam about twelve feet from the floor. She stared at it, and slowly she began to see three shadowy shapes twisting in a frenzied ballet as they pointed their toes, trying to reach the ground. She blinked, and the image disappeared. A trick of the light, she told herself.

"You saw the ghosts of the three men hanging there?" she asked the man.

"I don't see *ghosts.*" Sel paused as if aware that he had said too much. "My granddad and me, we saw real bodies hanging right there."

Marcie thought back to the somewhat rambling letter that *Roaming New England* had received from Sel. There had been a definite mention of ghosts. That was the only reason they had considered the story for their "Weird Happenings" column that covered paranormal events in New England. A multiple hanging alone wouldn't have gotten her out here. There had to be something supernatural.

"But you mentioned ghosts in your letter."

"Well, sure. But that came later, didn't it? I mean, they had to be dead first before they became ghosts."

"Okay," Marcie said, reminding herself to be patient. "So when did the ghosts show up?"

Sel looked off into the distance. "I was little when the hanging happened, only around five. I'm not exactly sure I know when that ghost business first started. But I can remember telling kids in school about folks' seeing ghosts of the men hanging in the barn. So I guess it started happening pretty much right after."

"Who saw them?"

Sel drifted off into his own world, then blinked and looked around as if surprised to see that they were alone.

"This was a lot busier place back in those days. That was during the war years, and we had all sorts of hired hands around then, mostly old guys and women of course."

"The war years?"

Sel stared at Marcie, then snorted. "Probably don't mean much to you, missy." His face saddened. "I'm talking about the big one."

"World War II?" Marcie asked.

He nodded.

"When did these hangings take place?"

"Back in July of '44."

"And later the people who worked here saw ghosts of these men hanging in the barn?" Marcie asked, wanting to make sure she had everything straight.

Sel nodded impatiently. "Yeah, but that's not the part I want to tell you about."

Marcie was about to say that *that* was the part she was interested in hearing, but she decided to stay with the soft approach. "What do you want to tell me about?" she asked.

"Why those men got hanged."

"That would be an interesting piece of local history," Marcie said slowly, "but I'm not sure it would make the kind of story we want."

"And I can tell you who did it. What do you think of that?" Sel said with a triumphant grin. "I know who did it. Nobody's known for over sixty years, but they've sure wondered. Now *I* know. Won't that make a story for your magazine?"

Solving an old crime could certainly be made to fit in the magazine somewhere, Marcie thought, but only if there were ghosts involved. A true crime and ghost story together would be a great combination.

Sel began talking again as if he'd forgotten that he'd

just asked her a question. "Nobody was here when it happened. My granddad and me had come back from fishing down at the stream. We went into the barn to put our gear away, and there they were. Granddad hustled me out pretty fast, but I saw them hanging right there." He pointed at the beam again. "Right there. Three of them, hanging in a row as neat as you please. Not a pretty sight, missy, I'll tell you that."

"I'll bet. But you didn't actually see the men being hanged?" Marcie asked.

"Wasn't anyone around at the time, except the guys that got hanged and the person who hanged them."

"I thought you said it was busy here back in those days."

"It was a Saturday afternoon in July. Granddad gave the men the afternoon off. My mom was in town at a meeting of the women's group at the church. That's why Granddad and me went off fishing."

"So why were those men killed?"

Sel made a cackling sound that Marcie guessed to be a laugh.

"You're a smart one, missy. Trying to get my story outta me with your smooth talk. But I'm smarter than that. This story is worth money." He rubbed his thumb and index finger together. "I'm not planning to just give it away."

"As I explained on the phone," Marcie said, taking a step back, "we pay two hundred dollars for a story idea that is eventually published."

A sly smile came over Sel's face. "I understand you folks from the big city. That's just a negotiating position.

You're hoping that a country bumpkin like me will give away the biggest story that ever came out of Doric for chicken feed. But I want you to know that I'm not planning to do that. We're talking something worth thousands of dollars here, not hundreds."

Marcie shook her head. Not sure whether she was more stunned by Sel's belief that Wells, Maine, the small town where the magazine was located, was a big city or by his confidence that she had thousands of dollars to throw around on story ideas.

"I'm sorry. Two hundred dollars is a firm offer. That's all we pay for any story."

Sel strutted toward her like a bantam rooster and waggled a finger at her. "Don't try to bluff me, missy. Because I just might call your bluff. I got proof to back up what I'm telling you. And there are other folks around who are gonna be real interested in what I have to say, and they'll pay me a damn sight more than two hundred dollars."

Marcie was about to make a sharp retort when she suddenly became aware that she was standing in an abandoned barn in the middle of nowhere, arguing with a man whose mental health was at least questionable. Although she was fit and sturdy and could probably handle Sel in a fair fight, Marcie decided that caution was probably wiser than confrontation. She edged sideways, glad that her eyes had adjusted well enough that she could make out a relatively clear path to the door.

"Go ahead. You just leave," Sel said, spotting her move and reaching out as if to shove her.

"Don't touch me," Marcie said in a low, angry voice.

Set's hand stopped in midair. Even in his hazy state of mind, something of Marcie's rage got through to him. "Then get out of here," he responded more hesitantly.

Not taking her eyes off him except to briefly glance over her shoulder to make sure she wasn't going to fall over some piece of farm machinery, Marcie backed out of the barn. Sel followed at a distance, watching her carefully. Probably making sure I didn't leave with a valuable piece of evidence, Marcie thought.

Once out of the barn, Marcie walked to her car, purposely slowing her gait so as not to show fear. Sel stayed a few yards away, sucking in his cheeks and looking puzzled, as if he couldn't figure out how things had gone so wrong.

As her hand closed around the door handle, he shouted, "You change your mind, you'd better get back to me by supper time. Else it's going to be too late."

Marcie started the engine and did a wide swing around the yard to head back to the lane. As she went past Sel, she gave him a casual wave to show that he hadn't rattled her. But as she slowly drove back down the narrow lane, she tightened her hands on the steering wheel to keep them from trembling.

Chapter Two

"I guess we can scratch that story," Amanda said, when Marcie called from the inn later in the afternoon and described her adventure.

"Unless you can come up with more money," Marcie said, hoping that her senior editor would find the resources to salvage the story.

Although she had left the Hayes farm relieved to be getting away from its weird owner, on the drive back the story had started to grow on her. This wasn't your average supernatural fantasy with little or no foundation in fact. Real men had died in that barn, and if Sel could be believed, the crime had never been solved.

"A few thousand." Amanda gave a short laugh. "You're talking about our travel and story budgets for the year."

"That's what I figured. Too bad, though."

"You think it might be a good story?"

"Sel Hayes did say that he had evidence to back up his claims."

"Sounds like a nutcase to me. Or at the very least an old guy who spends too much time alone on his farm, drinking and thinking about the past. Some of what he told you probably is accurate, but by now he's mixed the truth with his imagined version of what happened to the point where he doesn't know what's real and what isn't."

"I suppose."

"Hang on a second. I've got another call."

Marcie sighed and looked around her room. Unlike a lot of New England inns that went in for elaborate décor, trying to capture the sort of country chic so popular in home fashion magazines, the Doric Inn aimed for simplicity—*starkness* would actually be a more accurate word. A plain dresser with an attached mirror stood next to the one window, which was covered by a sheer curtain and a half-drawn shade. The bedside table, protected by a white linen scarf with aging yellowed lace around the edge, held a lamp and a twenty-year-old radio alarm clock. The bed that Marcie was lying on clearly emphasized firmness over comfort, as did the wooden chair that stood on the other side of the bed. A simple braided rug and a vase of dusty artificial flowers supplied the only embellishment. Doric was clearly not a tourist town.

"Sorry about that," Amanda said, returning to the line. "Without Greg here, things are a little frantic."

"Is he still down in Boston?"

"Yes. It looks as if the owners are serious about starting up a second magazine."

"I can't believe they think a culinary magazine featuring New England food would be a seller," Marcie said. "We could have just added a food column to *Roaming New England*."

"I feel the same way, but they did some sort of marketing survey that showed a magazine on New England regional cuisine would be a hit. I'm sure Greg will be back with us once they get the project up and running and hire a general editor. He's too much of a reporter to be happy with that kind of lifestyle stuff for very long."

"I hope so."

Amanda paused. "Traveling alone isn't much fun, is it?"

"Well, we did have pretty good times on the road together."

"Two cases of multiple murders in two trips. I wonder if 'good times' is precisely the right phrase."

Marcie snorted. "I guess you've got a point."

"You're all right, aren't you? Nothing happened with this guy that you're not telling me about?"

"Nope. I'm fine. He was just a little weird."

Marcie guessed that Amanda would have liked to offer her the option of canceling the rest of the trip and returning home. The six-year gap in their ages between Marcie's twenty-three and Amanda's twenty-nine was enough to make Amanda want to treat her like a younger sister. But Marcie knew that circumstances wouldn't allow Amanda that luxury, and, to be honest, Marcie knew it was time for her to start doing more on her own.

"Really, I'm fine," Marcie repeated, forcing a more upbeat tone.

"Okay. Why don't you give the guy with the next story on your list a call and see if you can reschedule that interview for tomorrow?"

"Yeah. That should work. I was planning to spend another day here gathering material for the Hayes farm story, but there's no point in doing that now. My next stop is about fifty miles north of Montpelier; that's only about eighty miles away from here. I'll see if I can move everything up and get back a day early to give you some help with editing the next issue."

"Sounds great."

After she said good-bye to Amanda, Marcie placed a call to the next person she was set to interview, and he agreed to see her the next afternoon. Since the numbers on the clock radio showed that it was only going on five, Marcie figured there was time to get some work done before heading down to the inn's restaurant for dinner. She opened her laptop and began reading over a story she'd been working on back at the office about a phantom dog that would allegedly howl the night before someone in the village died. Howling dogs in New England villages during the nineteenth century certainly weren't that uncommon, but a phantom dog that only appeared in front of the house of a person who was to die the next day was something special. As exciting as the story was, however, Marcie quickly found her early departure and long drive catching up with her as she struggled to stay awake.

Seldon Hayes also struggled to stay awake. In his case the problem was due more to the brown liquid in the glass in front of him than weariness. He looked at the man seated across from him and grinned broadly, exposing his toothless gums.

"I knew you were a smart businessman and wouldn't let an opportunity like this pass you by."

The man nodded and poured more whiskey into Sel's glass.

"And it's not like we're doing anything wrong. What we're hiding happened a long time ago, and even back then, it wasn't really the wrong thing to do, was it?"

The man gave an ambiguous shrug, as if such ethical distinctions were beside the point.

"What happened later, though, that was wrong," Sel said in a firmer voice and with a flash of anger in his eyes.

The man took a white envelope out of his jacket pocket. He stretched across the table and placed it squarely in front of Sel, so he'd have to reach over it for his glass. Sel seemed to debate for a moment whether to pick up the envelope or the glass next. Finally he opted for the envelope. He opened the flap and carefully fingered the bills.

"That's mighty generous of you. I'm not a greedy person, you understand. This will keep me very happy for the next month."

The man nodded.

Sel took a sip from his glass, and his eyes narrowed.

"I know you'd like to have my granddad's papers. Maybe someday when I know my time is coming I'd be willing to sell them to you, so I can have one big blast at the end. But you can see why I want to hang on to them for now, can't you? I don't have anything by way of a pension."

The man stared at him, unblinking. Sel began to feel a little uncomfortable and squirmed in his chair for a moment. He took another drink. A pleasant warmth coursed through his body. This must be really good whiskey, because he'd never felt this relaxed before, he thought, putting the glass to his lips again. Time skipped for a moment, and he realized that his eyes had closed. He tried to open them, but they seemed determined to stay shut. With a burst of effort, Sel returned the glass to the table, but it turned over as his chin sank down onto his chest.

The man quickly reached over and picked up the envelope of money before the puddle of barbiturate-laced whiskey could reach it. He put it back into his pocket and glanced out the window. He noted with approval that there were still several hours of daylight left. A good opportunity to do a quick preliminary search of the house from attic to cellar. He looked across at the old man, whose head now rested on his left arm. Sel would sleep peacefully for hours. There would be plenty of time to do the other thing after the search.

Marcie awoke with a start as she began to slide off the pillow placed against the headboard. She immediately sat bolt upright as if to show that she hadn't really been sleeping. "Sleep at night, not during the day," was one of her father's many commandments that he would punish her for disobeying. Even now she would still awaken from a nap in a panic to conceal that she had been sleeping.

She looked at the clock and saw that it was nearly six. Time to go down and get something to eat. Marcie rolled off the bed and straightened her clothes; then, standing in front of the mirror, she dragged a comb through her curly reddish brown hair. Barely glancing at the final result, she left her room, locking the door carefully behind her.

At the bottom of the stairs she passed the registration desk, then turned right into the dining room. A teenaged girl wearing a white blouse and black slacks greeted her and asked if she would be alone for dinner. Marcie nodded, feeling as if she were admitting to the world that no one was willing to dine with her. Even though she knew that tens of thousands of women were eating alone in public that very night for a variety of reasons, she couldn't shake off a sense of discomfort at having no companion. It made her feel lonely.

The hostess placed her at a table for two by a window that looked out onto the gravel parking lot and handed her the single sheet of paper that was the night's menu. Marcie quickly made her choice, then glanced around the room. There were about a dozen tables. Only two of them besides her own were occupied. An older couple sat at another table for two by the far window, and three women sat together on the other side of the room.

The waitress, a middle-aged woman who managed to be both efficient and pleasant, came by and wrote down her order of roast chicken, a baked potato, and salad. Once that was done, Marcie reached into her bag and took out a book. Reading while having dinner out by herself made her feel less conspicuous, and it was also an easy way of avoiding eye contact with strange men. However, the place was so empty, she didn't think that would be a problem tonight.

As if to prove her wrong, the hostess guided a man in his midtwenties into the room and seated him at the last remaining table for two, which was about ten feet in front of Marcie. Although the hostess tried to seat him so his back would be to Marcie, he scooted around the table and sat facing her. A quick glimpse told her that he was tall—several inches over six feet—and very thin. He wasn't exactly handsome, but he looked pleasant in an open, boyish sort of way. He also needed his light brown hair trimmed so that it didn't fluff over his ears and hang down across his forehead, Marcie decided.

She returned to her book, not wanting to get involved in a conversation with a stranger. But the story, which she had liked well enough up to then, no longer seemed to hold her attention. Her eyes kept drifting from the page up to the man's face. Since he was intently studying the menu, Marcie felt quite safe doing so. So safe, in fact, that when he glanced up and smiled, she was slow to look away.

"I'd ask you if you come here often, but I don't think anyone does," he said in a stage whisper.

Marcie found herself smiling. "I don't think many people even come here once," she replied in the same tone.

"Not unless they have a good reason."

"If your room is as basic as mine, it would have to be a very good reason," Marcie said, then suddenly panicked over whether that could be interpreted as a desire to see his room.

"What's your reason?" he asked.

"I'm here on business."

"What kind of business are you in?"

"I'm a magazine editor."

"Really? I'm a newspaper reporter," he said, then blushed and gave a disparaging shrug. "Well, I'm sort of a reporter. I'm a stringer actually. I work on a story-by-story basis for a paper in Montpelier, the *Courier.* Ever hear of it?"

Marcie shook her head. "I'm from the coast of Maine."

The man opened his mouth to say more, then paused.

"We could go on whispering across the distance, and I guess no one would notice."

They quickly surveyed the room in unison and saw that no one was paying attention to them. When their eyes met again, they both smiled.

"Like you said, not a bustling place," the man said. "But if you wouldn't mind, I could join you or you could join me. You'd be doing me a favor, because I didn't have the foresight to bring something to read, not even a copy of the *Courier,* which would give me seconds of reading pleasure."

Marcie grinned and waved in the direction of the chair across from her.

He grabbed his place setting and brought it with him. When he was seated, she put her hand across the table. "I'm Marcie Ducasse."

His long, thin fingers enveloped her hand. "Kevin Murray."

The waitress came into the room with two bread baskets in her hands and paused for a moment, figuring out the new arrangement. She came up to the table and placed both baskets down. "I guess you'll need both of these," she said with a smile.

Kevin ordered the pork chops and rice.

"I can hold your meal until his is ready if you'd like," she said to Marcie.

"You can start eating before me if you're hungry. I won't mind. I probably eat faster than you do," Kevin said.

"Bring mine when you bring his," Marcie said to the waitress, who nodded and hurried back toward the kitchen. "I kind of tuck into my food too," she explained to Kevin. "I don't think I'll need a head start."

"A woman after my own heart," he said with a disarmingly boyish grin.

"You don't look like a big eater."

"I've got a fast metabolism."

"Wish I did," Marcie said without thinking.

"You look fine to me," Kevin replied. He awkwardly pushed an unruly shock of hair off his forehead. "Sorry, that was out of line."

Marcie shook her head. "A genuine compliment is never out of line."

A large smile of relief went across his thin face, and he offered a basket of bread to Marcie.

"So, what magazine are you with?"

"Roaming New England."

"Sure. I know that one. They've got that great section, 'Weird Happenings,' with all that supernatural stuff."

"I write a lot of that," Marcie said, trying to keep the pride in her voice down to a minimum.

"You do?" His eyebrows disappeared into the comma of hair that had returned to his forehead.

"Yeah. Well, not by myself, of course. I'm only an associate editor. There's an editor and a managing editor above me."

"Still, better than being a part-timer. Although that's really my own fault."

"Why do you say that?" Marcie asked, spreading butter on a hot roll, then licking her fingers.

Kevin paused as if wondering whether he'd already said too much. He gave her a guilty smile. "My father is the owner of the *Courier.* He wants me to work my way up and take over from him someday."

"And he's starting you as a stringer?" Marcie said. "That's cruel."

Kevin laughed. "He'd put me on the staff full-time if I wanted. In fact, he'd be delighted to have me on board."

"So what's the problem?"

"For one thing, I'm not sure I want my father as my boss. Things are tough enough between us as it is."

"Yeah. It's not my favorite relationship either."

"So you've got a father around who always wants things done his way or else?"

"He's around somewhere, I guess."

Kevin stopped with a piece of roll halfway to his mouth. The closed expression on Marcie's face warned him not to pursue the matter.

"Plus, I figure that if I prove myself as a stringer, then if I do start working on the paper, people won't think I got the job just because of my father."

"Makes sense."

"Yeah. Except I don't make much money, so I still have to live at home with my folks. Even though I don't work directly for my father, I live under the same roof. You know how that works."

"My house, my rules," Marcie said.

"Exactly. Sometimes I think it would be better to work *for* him, so I didn't have to live *with* him."

The waitress brought their salads, and they began to eat. Over the course of the meal Marcie told him about going to Boston University, living out west on Army bases, and working on a magazine. He told her about going to Bowdoin College, playing lacrosse, and being the only child of a man who was determined to see his son walk in his footsteps. By the time they'd finished with a dessert of chocolate cake, Marcie felt she knew Kevin Murray pretty well. Well enough, anyway, to suggest that they get together for breakfast.

Later, as she got ready for bed, Marcie felt a pang of regret that she and Kevin didn't live closer to each other. He seemed like an interesting guy, but a four-hour drive was too much of a test for any budding relationship. Her mind was coming up with various creative scenarios to solve that problem when she drifted off to sleep.

Chapter Three

Marcie opened her eyes when the first milky slivers of light worked their way around the edges of the shade covering her one window. She awoke feeling happy, but it took her an instant to recall the reason. As soon as she remembered her breakfast meeting with Kevin, she bounded out of bed and slipped down the hall to the bathroom she shared with the other two rooms on her end of the hall. She and Kevin had agreed to meet when the dining room opened for breakfast at seven. Marcie was glad that Kevin was on the floor above, so there was no chance of running into him in the hall before she'd gotten herself organized.

A half hour later she was ready, and it was only a quarter to seven. Marcie waited nervously in her room for five minutes, not wanting to appear overly eager, then figured the heck with it and decided to go downstairs and sit in the lobby until the dining room opened. As she came down to the first floor, Marcie saw Barbara Sharp, the woman who ran the inn, standing behind the reception desk talking to a bald man wearing a suit. Hovering behind Mrs. Sharp was her mother, Mrs. Evans, who had given Marcie the directions to Sel Hayes' farm yesterday afternoon. As Marcie came down the stairs, the older woman gave her a worried glance.

"Ah, here she is now, Chief," Barbara Sharp said loudly with obvious relief in her voice.

The man turned to Marcie and nodded. He was heavy-set with a round, babyish face. His bushy eyebrows produced a striking contrast to his almost completely hairless head.

"I'm Pat Roylston, the chief of police in Doric. I was just asking Mrs. Sharp if she'd be willing to go upstairs and see if you'd be able to come down and talk to me. Fortunately now that you're here, that won't be necessary."

"What do you want to talk to me about?" Marcie asked, her stomach flip-flopping at the thought of being involved with the police once again.

The man ignored Marcie's question and turned to Mrs. Sharp's mother. "Is this the woman you gave directions to yesterday?"

The older woman looked as if she wished she didn't have to answer. "Yes, it is," she slowly replied with all the solemnity of someone on the witness stand.

"Why don't we go where we can discuss this in private?" Roylston said to Marcie. With a wave of his hand, he gestured toward the empty lobby.

"Discuss what?" Marcie asked.

Roylston didn't answer but directed her more emphatically toward the lobby.

Marcie reluctantly went into the lobby and settled into a love seat that had seen better days. Roylston pulled over a wooden chair, so he was facing her with his back to the main desk. He took out a notebook and a pen.

"What time was it that you got directions to the Hayes farm?"

"As I'm sure Mrs. Evans has already told you, it was just a little after three o'clock."

"Did you go out to the farm directly from here?"

"That's right."

"What time did you arrive?"

"I don't know exactly. But I didn't stop along the way, and I'm sure you know how long it takes to get from here to the farm."

Marcie knew that being rude to the police probably never paid, but she didn't take well to men who refused to answer her questions.

"And you saw Seldon Hayes when you arrived at the farm?"

"Yes."

"Why did you go to the farm?"

Marcie told the chief about her job and summarized Sel's letter describing his story.

"So you wanted to write about the hangings?"

"Not exactly. I wanted to write about the ghosts."

One of the bushy eyebrows rose in an exaggerated expression of surprise.

"That's what my column in *Roaming New England*

Magazine is all about, paranormal events in New England."

The chief paused and stared at Marcie for a moment while he tapped the top of his pen on the notebook. Marcie figured that he was wondering whether he was interviewing some kind of kook.

"What happened when you arrived at the farm?"

Marcie described going into the barn and what Sel had said about the hangings.

"After you heard what he said, did you decide to write a story about the Hayes farm?"

"I wanted to, but it didn't work out."

"Why not?"

"Sel wanted a lot of money for the story, and we couldn't pay nearly as much as he wanted."

"So you had an argument?"

"I wouldn't call it an argument. Mr. Hayes was unhappy that I wouldn't pay more. So we decided to end our discussion of the project."

During her short time in publishing, Marcie had frequently heard editors talking about "ending a discussion of a project." She liked the professional sound of it.

"And after that?" the chief asked.

"I got into my car and left."

"Where was Sel at that time?"

"Standing in the yard in front of the farmhouse, watching me leave."

"Was anyone else there?"

"I didn't see anyone."

The chief made a note on his pad. He looked across

the room, and his bushy eyebrows drew together as he formulated another question. "Are you sure nothing more happened?" he asked.

"Like what?" Marcie snapped.

"Everyone knows that Sel was a little strange. Maybe he got fresh or tried to touch you in some inappropriate way? Possibly he even became violent. No one could blame you if you reacted to a physical assault of some kind."

The lines in the chief's face smoothed out in what Marcie guessed was his most sympathetic expression.

"He got angry when I wouldn't pay him what he wanted, but it never got physical. Has something happened to him? Is that why you're asking me all these questions?"

"He's dead," the chief said, watching her face carefully.

"Dead? How? He was fine when I saw him yesterday."

"That's why I'm asking you these questions—because as far as we know, you were the last person to talk to him before he died."

"That's not exactly true, Chief," a man's voice said.

Marcie had been so busy studying the chief's face that she hadn't seen Kevin walk up behind him. The chief stood and turned to face the young man. He didn't seem happy to find that he was half a foot shorter than Kevin.

"Who are you?"

"Kevin Murray. I work for the *Courier*." He put out his hand, and the chief reluctantly took it. "I know that Sel Hayes is dead because the paper gave me a call this morning letting me know. He was found hanging in the barn, right?"

The chief ignored his question. "How do you know that Ms. Ducasse wasn't the last person to talk to Hayes?"

"Because I called him on the phone after Ms. Ducasse returned to the inn."

"What time did you talk to him?"

"Four-thirty. Right after Ms. Ducasse got back." He gave her a guilty sidelong look.

"Are you related to Howard Murray, the owner of the *Courier*?" Roylston asked.

Kevin nodded, looking uncomfortable. "He's my father."

"I heard him speak at a meeting of the Vermont Police Chiefs' Association. Why don't you pull up another chair, and we'll all sit down? Then you can both tell me what you know about this," the chief suggested.

Kevin dragged another wooden chair over and sat next to Marcie, trying to avoid the angry, puzzled glance she was giving him.

"Where would you like me to start?" asked Kevin.

"The beginning is always good," the chief replied.

"Okay. Well, I had heard from a contact of mine in town that Sel Hayes was looking for someone to buy his story. Of course, I knew about the story of the hanged men already. Anyone from around the region with any interest in history has heard something about it. But this was the first time Sel had let on that he knew anything about who committed the murders."

"Your contact," the chief said with heavy emphasis. "Who would that be?"

Kevin paused.

"And I don't want to hear about privileged sources. This isn't Washington."

Kevin shrugged. "Jack Brill, the bartender at The Lonesome Pine, Sel's favorite watering hole."

"So you came to town because you wanted to get this story for your paper?" the chief asked.

Marcie stiffened in her chair and glared at Kevin. "Did you know that I was going to be here?" she asked before Kevin could answer the chief's question.

Kevin blushed. "Actually, I did know. Sel has told anyone in the bar who would listen for the last two weeks that he had this woman from a big magazine coming into town to buy his story."

"Were you at the inn when I asked for directions?" she asked, remembering how she had felt watched.

"I was sitting in the lounge. I just happened to hear you introduce yourself and ask how to get to the Hayes place."

" '*Just happened*,' " Marcie said with sarcasm. "You mean you were spying on me."

Kevin's long body squirmed in the chair. "I had called Sel, and he told me when you were coming and that you were going to stay here. He said that if he couldn't make a deal with you, he might consider talking to me. I guess he figured that a regional magazine would be able to come up with more money than a local newspaper."

"Was he ever wrong," Marcie mumbled. "Were you really going to pay him thousands of dollars for his story?"

"Of course not. My dad would never approve that kind of expenditure. When I talked to Sel after you got back to the inn, I offered him four hundred. That was the most I was going to be able to scrape out of our special fund for sources. And I told him it would have to be a great story that would run for several issues for me to even come up with that."

"What did he say?" Roylston asked, trying to get back control of the interview.

"That he expected to have a better offer on the table in an hour."

"Did he say any more than that?"

Kevin shook his head. "I figured he was just stringing me along to get more money."

"I guess you were way wrong about that," Marcie said. "I'd say that he did have another buyer, and whoever it was killed him." She turned to the chief. "Was he hanged from that beam like the others?"

"From what I understand, the circumstances are similar," the chief admitted.

"You couldn't have seriously thought that I'd strung up the guy," Marcie said.

The chief gave her a bland look. "I was simply trying to establish what you observed at the time."

As Marcie opened her mouth to say more, Roylston held up a hand. "Look, we're getting way ahead of ourselves. I doubt that we've even got a murder here. Sel probably committed suicide. Living out there all alone, he'd be pretty remarkable if he didn't get depressed, and he was always going on about the hangings. So it's not surprising that that's the route he would follow. We even found a stepladder just out of range of his feet, like he'd kicked it over."

"So you think he tied a rope to the beam, went up on

the ladder, put his head through the noose, then kicked the ladder away?" Kevin asked.

The chief nodded.

"He didn't sound depressed to me when I saw him that afternoon. He sounded greedy but not depressed," Marcie said.

"Yeah, he seemed the same way to me when I talked to him on the phone," Kevin added. "If Sel was planning to do himself in, he wouldn't have been wheeling and dealing with me an hour before."

"Did he leave a note?" Marcie asked.

The chief shook his head. "But not every suicide does."

"Sounds like murder to me," Kevin said.

"But if it was murder, how was it done?" Marcie asked. "It seems to me that it would be hard to hang someone while he was still alive. Maybe he was already unconscious or dead?"

"There were no signs of trauma other than the hanging," the chief said.

"Weren't those guys who were killed years ago drugged first?" asked Kevin. "I seem to remember hearing something about that."

The chief nodded. "I looked over the old file first thing this morning. All three of them were drugged before they were hanged. They had alcohol and barbiturates in their systems."

"When will you know whether that's true for Sel?" Kevin asked.

"It will be at least a week before the lab tests are complete. Sel smelled of alcohol, but then, he probably always did."

"So it could be the same killer," Kevin said, his eyes lighting up at the thought of a good story. "He killed Sel because he was threatening to reveal what happened back then."

"I doubt it's the same guy," Marcie objected. "That happened over sixty years ago. Unless the killer was a kid when he committed the first crime, he'd be at least in his eighties by now. Not many guys that age are fit enough to go around hanging people. What do you think, Chief?"

Roylston cleared his throat, obviously not happy about being questioned. "All I can tell you is that the three men who were murdered years ago were carried up to the hayloft, had nooses placed around their necks, and then were pushed off. Their necks were broken by the fall. We don't have the report yet on whether Sel's neck was broken, and, as I said, it was most likely a suicide. But I guess that if he were killed in the same way, it would have taken a fit individual to carry an unconscious person up to the hayloft."

"Sel wasn't very big," Kevin pointed out.

"All the same," Marcie said stubbornly, "you're talking about a geriatric murderer."

"Same method, same guy," Kevin shot back.

Marcie shook her head. "Apparently everyone around here knows how it was done. Even *you* knew that. It could be a copycat."

The chief cleared his throat. "As much as I'd like to sit here listening to the two of you speculate all morning, I have an unexplained death to investigate, so I'd better get going. Can both of you stay in town for the next couple of days?"

"I really need to get on to my next interview," Marcie said. "I was planning to leave this morning."

"And I can't afford to stay here for two more nights," Kevin said. "I'm paying my own way."

The chief's right eyebrow twisted upward. "I thought your father owned the *Courier*?"

"It's a long story," Kevin said with a sigh.

"Well, let me explain things to you. As far as I know, you are the only two people who talked to Seldon Hayes yesterday, and until I have a better sense of what happened, I'd like to have both of you here where I can reach you. Consider yourselves material witnesses, and stay in town."

"Do we have a choice?" Marcie asked.

The chief smiled. "I suppose you could hire a lawyer and see if I can legally detain you. But it would probably take a couple of days to work it all out, and by then you'll be free to go."

"Great," Marcie said. "What am I supposed to do while I'm stranded in Doric, Vermont?"

The chief got to his feet. "There's some beautiful scenery around here. Or maybe the two of you could speculate some more on who killed old Sel. If you come up with any good ideas, let me know."

Marcie glared at Kevin. "I don't plan to even talk to *him*. Can't I charge him with stalking? He was spying on me."

"Look on the bright side. Mrs. Sharp told me that the two of you had dinner here last night. You might even be able to alibi each other for the time of death, once it's established."

"See? I'm your alibi," Kevin said with a bright smile.

"One more question, Chief," Marcie said, ignoring Kevin. "How did you happen to find Sel's body so quickly? That farm didn't look as if it got a lot of visitors."

"He didn't show up for work last night. His boss tried to call him, and when there was no answer, he went out to the farm."

"Sel had a job? Wasn't he pretty old for that?" Marcie asked. "He must have been in his late seventies."

"Only sixty-nine."

"He looked older," she said.

"He'd lived hard. And I imagine he needed the money to pay the taxes on the farm. I doubt that Sel was ever much of a saver."

"What kind of work did he do?"

"He worked from six to nine at the local farm-and-garden store a few nights a week."

"When did his boss find the body?" Kevin asked.

"Around eight. On his way home from work."

"So he died somewhere between when I called him at four-thirty and eight," Kevin concluded. Then he looked at Marcie and smiled. "We probably *were* having dinner when it happened."

"Don't remind me."

"I'll leave the two of you for now," the chief said, standing. "Try to play nice."

Chapter Four

"Don't go!" Kevin said.

As soon as the chief left the room, Marcie stood and started to exit the lobby. She'd do without breakfast rather than have it with Kevin, now that he had proven himself to be a liar and a sneak.

Kevin quickly blocked her way. "Look, I apologize for what I did, but you have to give me a chance to explain."

"I don't want to hear your pitiful excuses for lying to me."

Kevin pushed the hair off his forehead and blushed.

"And don't give me that 'aw, shucks' look," Marcie snapped. "Go get a haircut."

"I understand why you're angry. And maybe in some ways what I did wasn't quite up-front—"

"Not up-front?" Marcie almost shouted, then lowered her voice. "It was downright deceptive. What kind of a reporter hides the fact from a fellow journalist that he's working on the same story?"

"Actually, I think that happens quite a bit. But last night I didn't ask you anything about your story, did I? I didn't pump you for information."

Marcie opened her mouth to respond, then paused. It was true that although their discussion had ranged widely over their respective pasts and likes and dislikes, Kevin had never once asked her for any specifics about why she was in town. Her vague statement that she was research-ing a story had been enough for him.

"You already knew why I was here."

"True. But I didn't know exactly what Sel had said to you. Knowing how much you had offered him might have helped me in my negotiations. And I didn't try to find out what he told you about the hanged men."

"Probably you were waiting to find out more over breakfast," Marcie replied, refusing to budge. "And I can't forgive you for spying on me."

"I wasn't spying, not really. I knew you were going to be here, that's true, but I had to remain in town too, in case Sel was willing to talk to me. There's only one place in Doric to stay. I just happened to be in the lobby when you stopped by for directions. It was kismet."

Marcie snorted. "You followed me out to the farm."

"No, I didn't. I stayed right in the lobby. I was still sitting there when you came back."

"So you could give Sel a call and top my offer," Mar-cie said with a note of triumph, as if Kevin's shiftiness had been conclusively proven.

Kevin sighed and brushed the hair off his forehead. "You're right, I should get it get cut," he said, grinning.

Marcie had to force herself not to grin back.

"Look, it's true, I did know we were in competition for the same story, but that wasn't why I had dinner with you last night. You just seemed to be a person I'd like to get to know. The fact that we were interested in the same story had nothing to do with it."

Marcie gave him a skeptical look but could feel herself weakening. "So you weren't the least bit interested in finding out what Seldon Hayes had told me about the hangings?"

"I was interested, but I resisted asking about it. I was more interested in getting to know you."

"Had you really heard about my 'Weird Happenings' column like you said?"

"Not until last week," Kevin admitted. "Once I heard you were coming to town, I did read back issues of the magazine. And I was honestly impressed by your column."

Marcie paused and looked across the lobby, wondering whether she should accept his apology. She knew she tended to be overly suspicious of men, and what Kevin had said was somewhat convincing. But she was definitely going to be more cautious with him from now on.

Kevin studied her face. "Are we friends again?" he asked with a tentative smile.

Marcie put out her hand. "Provisional friends. Trick me again, and it's over for good. You're on probation."

Kevin gave her hand a firm shake. "Good. Now we should get to work," he said.

"At what?"

"At finding out what happened to Seldon Hayes. There's a big story here. Big enough that we can each have a piece of it."

"But this is a police investigation. We can't get involved."

"The chief virtually invited us to get involved. He told us to speculate about who committed the crime. Doesn't that give us a free hand to investigate?"

Marcie grinned. "I'm not sure they're the same thing, and I think he was only kidding."

Kevin gave her a light punch on the shoulder. "C'mon, what are we going to do here otherwise? We can't leave Doric for a couple of days. We may as well put the time to good use."

She looked at his face. He seemed so enthusiastic and confident. All the boyish fumbling had disappeared, replaced by a self-assured professionalism. Marcie found herself wanting to go along. She missed Amanda. Being part of a team again might be fun.

"Okay. Where do we start?"

"First of all, why don't you tell me what Sel said about the hangings?"

"Now wait a minute."

Kevin put a hand to his heart. "The essence of teamwork is trust. Am I right?"

"I suppose."

"So why don't you tell me all about your adventure down on the farm over breakfast? After that we'll find our way to the local library to do some research on Sel's story. Does that sound good?"

Marcie found herself being gently guided toward the dining room before she had a chance to object.

They decided over a hearty breakfast that Sel's death must have something to do with the story of the three hangings, as neither of them considered suicide to be a likely scenario. Kevin still favored the idea that the original killer had struck again to conceal his identity, while Marcie didn't think that was possible because of his age. However, they agreed that they had to find out more about the events surrounding the original murders in order to discover why Sel had been killed.

Kevin suggested that the best place to start their research was with back issues of the *Courier* from the time of the hangings. The last ten years of the *Courier* were online, Kevin explained, but to get issues before that they'd have to hope the library kept them on microfiche. If they didn't, he could get someone back in Montpelier to check in the paper's morgue and make copies of relevant articles. But that would take time, so they decided to try the library first.

Doric's library, an ornate stone building next to the elementary school and across the street from the town hall, was two blocks away. As they passed under an arch to get to the door, Marcie thought how much it looked like a castle built to defend the books from barbarians. Kevin pulled open the door made of thick glass set in a heavy iron frame. Across the short entryway was the front desk. Windows cut high in a wall let in some light, while the rest of the illumination was supplied from old ceiling fixtures hanging down like stalactites. The yellowish incandescent light combined with the rich wood moldings gave the room the sepia cast of an old photo.

Marcie expected to see an equally old woman at the desk with glasses hanging from a cord around her neck and a pinched expression, but the person who looked up at them and smiled cheerfully was a cute brunet no older than herself.

"Can I help you?" she asked, focusing most of her attention on Kevin, who turned red when she smiled at him.

"Do you have the *Courier* from 1944?" Kevin asked, giving her a shy smile of his own.

The young woman wrinkled her nose as if anything from that long ago would inevitably smell bad. "Gee, I don't know. I haven't worked here long, and nobody's ever asked me for a newspaper from way back then. But we do have the *Courier* down in the basement on microfiche." She glanced around the room. "The thing is, I'm all by myself right now, and I'm not supposed to leave the desk. It's kind of a silly rule, but they're a stickler for rules around here."

"I understand how that can be," Kevin said with a sympathetic smile. Suddenly his face became sad. Marcie thought he looked like a basset hound that had lost its bone.

"My problem is that I've just started a new job, and my first assignment in to do this research. This guy I work for is one of those 'accept no excuses' types, and he wants this information, like, yesterday."

Marcie could see the woman's brown eyes starting to melt. "I know how that is," she said. "The people around here treat me like a slave too."

The woman looked at Marcie, and her eyes hardened. Marcie realized that she was getting in the way of Kevin's attempt to sweet-talk his way into the microfiche stash.

"I'm just an intern," Marcie said quickly. "I'm along to take notes for Mr. Murray." She nodded deferentially toward Kevin as if she could never aspire to be more than his lowly assistant.

Kevin stuck his hand across the desk. "Sorry, I should have introduced myself. I'm Kevin Murray. This is my intern, Ms. Ducasse."

"Lisa Starr," the woman replied, taking his hand in a lingering grip. "I'd really like to help you, but, like I said, I'd be dead if they found I'd left the desk."

"How would they know, if you're the only employee here?" Marcie asked.

"They call at all hours just to check that I answer the phone," Lisa replied, not taking her eyes off Kevin.

Kevin nodded and rubbed his chin. "I see the problem. What if one of us went down to the basement and got the microfiche? Then you could stay right here at the desk in case they called."

"It's pretty dark down there, and there are all cobwebs and stuff. But I can tell you where to go if you'd like to look," she said, staring directly at Marcie.

I'd like to tell you where to go too, Marcie thought.

Kevin gave Marcie an imploring look.

"Sure, I'll go," Marcie said putting on a phony, eager-to-please expression. "Nothing I'd like better than being down there with all those 'cobwebs and stuff.' "

The sarcasm was lost on Lisa, who explained how

the rows of shelves were labeled and where she would find the microfiche of the *Courier.*

"They're in a bunch of dusty black boxes at the end of the shelf near the back wall. Rattle them around a little bit before you do anything. Last time I was down there, a mouse ran along the top when I took one out. I screamed so loud, the janitor almost called the police."

"Swell," Marcie said, glaring at Kevin. "How do I get to the basement?" Lisa pointed to a door at the far end of the room. Marcie walked across the reading room. It seemed to be empty except for a couple of old men who were sitting in a corner reading newspapers.

Marcie opened the door and found the switch that turned on a dim light over the stairs. The basement had smooth cement floors and walls but smelled so much of dampness that she wondered about the condition of the stuff stored down there. She found the row of shelves that contained the microfiche. Everything had been neatly labeled, and she easily discovered the box with the film from the year she wanted. After shaking the box around enough to scare a battalion of rodents, she slowly pulled it out and opened it. Sel had said that the hangings happened in July of 1944, so she removed the film canisters for that month and for the next two months, just to play it safe.

She got back to the front desk in time to see Lisa hand Kevin a piece of paper that he quickly folded and stashed in his shirt pocket.

"You can use the projector in the back of the reference section. The directions are posted on the wall," Lisa said to Kevin, reaching across the desk to touch his hand.

"Biggest mouse I ever saw," Marcie said softly, looking stunned.

"What?" Lisa's eyes grew wide. "Do you think it could have been a rat?" she asked in a whisper.

Marcie frowned. "Or a small cat."

Lisa's hand reached out blindly for the telephone. "I'm going to call the town hall. They need to get an exterminator over here."

"Good idea," Marcie said.

"Was there really a rat?" Kevin asked as he and Marcie walked side by side to the back of the reference section.

"I thought I smelled one. Did little Lisa just give you her telephone number?"

Kevin nodded sheepishly. "I didn't ask for it. But I couldn't very well refuse and hurt her feelings."

"Must be a terrible thing, having all that natural charm."

"It's not charm exactly. Women just seem to want to mother me."

Marcie thought of her own initial reaction and realized that he was probably right. She wondered if wanting to mother a man was a good basis for a long-term relationship.

"But you use it to your advantage," she said.

Kevin gave a guilty smile. "Only in the cause of journalism. And I haven't done that with you."

Marcie warned herself to stay on the alert to that possibility as she tossed him the two film containers. "Why don't you see if you can set up the microfiche projector, sonny?"

A few minutes later Kevin was leafing through old copies of the *Courier.*

"The whole format of the paper was different back then," he said, staring at a front page. "My grandfather was in charge in those days. He used to tell me that the paper was at its best before television."

"He probably thought that way because it's when he was in charge."

Kevin smiled. "Yeah. He never cared much for the changes Dad introduced."

"Sounds like your father had similar problem to yours when he was the same age."

"Yeah," Kevin said with a note of surprise in his voice. "I guess he did."

Kevin began flipping through the pages faster and faster. They flew by on the viewing screen: day by day, week by week. Marcie felt her stomach lurch. She turned away and sat down.

Kevin gave a low whistle that brought Marcie to her feet, looking over his shoulder.

"This was front-page news," he said, pointing to the bold headlines across the top of the July 21 edition. *Men Hanged in Barn* it read. Underneath, in only slightly smaller letters, it said, *Mass Murder Comes to Doric.*

When they finished reading the story, Kevin put a couple of coins into the side of the machine. It was attached to an old copier. Slowly a blurred image of the page curled out.

"Let's find out how the investigation turned out," Kevin said, turning the microfiche forward.

For the first few days after the hangings, the murders

remained headline news. Jack McDermott, the chief of police in Doric at the time, kept assuring people that his department, along with the help of the state police, was carrying out a vigorous investigation. But as the days went by and nothing much new was reported, the story slid farther back into the paper, replaced first by war news, then by other local events. By the end of ten days they could only find a small article on the bottom of the second page announcing that the funerals of the three victims were scheduled for the end of the week. Kevin reeled the film along until he found the obituaries and printed out copies.

Finally he sat back and took out a notebook that Marcie thought looked very similar to Chief Roylston's.

"Okay, what do we know?" he asked.

"Well, Sel's story seems to check out as far as it goes. His mother was in town the afternoon of the murders. He and his grandfather had gone down to the creek to fish and spent the afternoon there."

"About a quarter of a mile away from the farm, so they wouldn't have heard anything," Kevin added, scribbling in his notebook.

"And when they came back, the three men were hanging in the barn. Three local men from right here in Doric."

"But," Kevin said, raising his index finger for significance, "no one knows why they were at the farm. Sel's grandfather claimed to have no idea what they could have been doing in the barn."

Marcie frowned. "In a small town like this, you'd think that somebody would have known. You'd figure that at least one of these guys would have told his family or friends where he was going and why. Unless . . ."

"Unless it was something illegal or at least potentially embarrassing," Kevin said, finishing her thought. "Hey, maybe these guys were out there to start up some kind of criminal enterprise. After all, that farm is in a pretty remote spot, so maybe they thought it would be a good location for hiding stolen goods."

Marcie shook her head. "According to Sel, the farm was a busy place back then. The only reason no one was around at the time of the murders was because they'd been given the day off."

Kevin shrugged. "Okay. All three of these guys were single. Maybe they decided to get wild. They knew no one would be around at the farm, so they went there to meet up with some women. Could be they planned to have a little party on a warm summer afternoon."

"And then what—the women turned mean and decided to hang them?" Marcie asked.

"Angry boyfriends showed up?" Kevin suggested.

Marcie shook her head. "All three of these guys were drugged before they were hanged. Somebody planned this out carefully. Somebody who knew that the men were going to be at the farm and could guarantee that no one else would be around."

"Well, the farm belonged to Sel's grandfather," Kevin said. "Technically his father ran the place, but he was away in the Army at the time."

"What about the grandfather?" Marcie said. "Maybe he left Sel alone by that stream for a while or gave the boy something so he fell asleep. That might have given him enough time to come back to the barn to drug and hang those guys."

"He was close to sixty at the time."

"Yeah, but he worked on the farm. He might have been strong enough."

"I guess, but there's still a problem."

"What?"

"He only had one arm. He'd been in some kind of a farm accident when he was a kid."

Marcie stared for a moment. "How do you know that? It wasn't in the newspaper."

Kevin smiled shyly. "My contacts."

"Your famous contacts again. I'm surprised that you don't have this whole thing solved, with all that excellent information you have."

"My contact is really only one guy, the bartender at The Lonesome Pine. Sel used to go on a lot about how good a fisherman his granddad was, considering he had only one arm."

"Then I can see why the police didn't suspect him."

Kevin sighed. "So we've got three guys who were murdered together. They must have had something in common other than being locals."

Marcie flattened out the copies of the obituaries on the library table and studied them.

"They ranged in age from twenty-two to twenty-five. They all lived in town. They were all single."

She glanced up and saw a puzzled expression on Kevin's face.

"Something wrong?"

"They had another thing in common."

"What?"

"It was the middle of World War II."

"So?"

"They were all young, single guys, and not one of them was in the military."

Marcie frowned and stared at the scarred surface of the oak library table. She wondered how much less battered it had been back in 1944. Probably not much, given that the furniture looked as if it might be original to the building and the cornerstone said it had been finished in 1888.

"What are you saying? Do you think somebody was angry because these guys hadn't been drafted, so he decided to kill them?"

"Possibly," Kevin said with a shrug. "Or there could be something more to it than that. We won't know unless we investigate further."

Marcie felt a renewed sense of anxiety about getting involved in a police investigation. Her past efforts along that line had almost gotten her killed twice before, and she was in no hurry to risk her life again.

"I'll be back in a minute," Kevin said. He walked toward the front of the library.

Marcie studied the names listed on the obituary page: Matthew Carter, George Fuller, and Jacob Heller. Typical names of men who apparently, according to the few paragraphs that summed them up, had lived short but typical lives. Carter had worked on the family farm, Fuller worked in a bank, and Heller had a job in a garage. They were probably pretty representative of Doric or any other

Glen Ebisch

small town at the time. Young guys who today might go to college and move on to bigger cities, Marcie thought. Back then people stayed closer to home.

"Here we go," Kevin said, opening a phone book on the table. "This covers the region. One way to start is to talk to relatives of the victims."

"If any of them are still in the area."

Kevin opened the book to the *H*'s, and his finger went down the column.

"Bingo. We've got a Rachel Heller listed right here in Doric. She's probably related in some way." He flipped toward the front of the book. "Nothing under Fuller." He went back a few more pages. "But we do have six Carters to check out."

He pulled the cell phone off his belt and, with one eye on the phone book, began putting in numbers. The first two numbers didn't answer. The third claimed not to know anything about a Matthew Carter. But on the fourth call he must have gotten someone more helpful, because Marcie heard him introduce himself as a reporter for the *Courier*. From what she could pick up from his end of the conversation, he was talking to a to a woman named Sarah Carter. He told her about the death of Seldon Hayes. He made it sound as if he was doing an article on the history of the farm and wanted to include something about the murdered men. He ended the conversation by scheduling an appointment for right after lunch.

"Who was that?" Marcie asked.

"Sarah Carter, the wife of Philip Carter. He was Matt Carter's younger brother. He inherited the family farm when Matt died. He's dead now too. Died five years

ago. She sold the farm and lives in an assisted-living facility right outside of Montpelier. I'm going to see her
this afternoon."

"I'm surprised that she's willing to talk to you."

Kevin smiled. "Older people are always happy to
have someone to talk to, especially about the past."

"I guess. But this involves a kind of ugly story from
her family's past."

"Not her family, her husband's. I've found that a lot of
older women don't see their husband's family as their
own. Some of them are even happy to air that dirty laun-
dry, especially if they're widows."

He handed her his cell phone. "Your turn. Give this
Rachel Heller a call. See if she'll talk to you."

Marcie frowned. She felt a bit stunned by the speed
with which Kevin was pursuing the investigation. She'd
done some investigating with Amanda, and she'd certainly researched stories about the supernatural. But that
had been library research, with an occasional interview
with a would-be contributor. This was turning into professional journalism. She was an editor and writer, not a
journalist. But as she looked up at Kevin's eager face, she
felt challenged and didn't want to back down.

"What should I say to her?"

"Pretty much the truth. Tell her that you're planning to
write a story for your magazine about the three hanged
men." Kevin smiled. "If it sounds like she's about to hang
up, tell her that the story will be tasteful and show her family in a good light."

Marcie put in the number. The voice that answered
was such a dull monotone that at first Marcie thought she

had gotten an answering machine. But when she halt-ingly explained her reason for the call, the voice took on new emotion.

"I'm glad that someone has decided to expose the truth about what happened to my brother," the woman snapped. "My brother was murdered, and nobody in this godfor-saken town cared. It's about time they felt the hand of God's wrath."

Marcie caught her breath and managed to set up a meeting with her in about an hour at her home.

"So?" Kevin asked when she hung up. "Do you think she'll have much to say?"

"I think that's a safe bet," Marcie replied.

Chapter Five

Marcie stood by her car and took a deep breath. The morning had already been a busy one. First being questioned in a murder, then discovering that a potential boyfriend was something more and less than he appeared, and now embarking on a murder investigation. She had also been forced to reschedule her travel plans and interviews once again. When Marcie had called the man she was supposed to interview that afternoon to postpone their appointment, he had been a bit put out. However, when she explained the cause of her delay, he had happily forgiven her in exchange for a promise that she would tell him all about it when she saw him in a few days' time. She only hoped there would be a good story to tell.

Marcie looked up at the Heller house, a medium-sized white clapboard. It had a fresh-looking coat of paint. The lawn was neatly mowed, the flower gardens carefully tended. Since Rachel Heller had to be a rather elderly woman, Marcie figured that she must be able to afford to hire someone to do the maintenance. But, if the phone conversation had been any indication, having money apparently hadn't made the woman any less angry, and it was with some trepidation that Marcie went up the walk to the front door and rang the bell.

The door opened the few inches that the safety chain allowed, and a pair of eyes peered out directly into her own.

"Ms. Heller?" Marcie asked, not being able to make out a face.

"*Miss* Heller. Are you the one from the magazine?" a firm voice asked.

When Marcie answered in the affirmative, the door closed, and she heard the chain being undone. When the door opened again, not much wider than the first time, a thin hand appeared in the space to motion her inside with a crooked finger.

Marcie turned sideways to enter. As her eyes adjusted to the darkened hallway, she heard the door shut behind her and the chain slide back into place.

"Neighbors always want to know your business. They're not going to find out any of mine," the woman muttered. "Turn left into the living room."

Marcie did as she was told and found herself in a large, shadowy room filled with furniture.

"Sit over there," the woman said, pointing toward a pale blue sofa. "That way I can see you when I'm in my favorite chair."

Marcie sat, and Miss Heller settled into a wing chair that looked far too uncomfortable to be anyone's favorite. The woman perched on the edge of the seat across from Marcie was thin and fidgety, ready to leap to her feet at any moment. Her gray hair was held tightly in place by a complicated arrangement of combs, and she was wearing a dress that to Marcie's eye looked rather formal for the occasion, more what someone might wear to church on Sunday.

"You claim that you work for a magazine," she said in a tone that indicated being lied to was an everyday occurrence.

"*Roaming New England Magazine,*" Marcie answered.

"Never heard of it. That doesn't sound like the sort of publication that would be interested in a murder. Is it one of those fancy magazines that are full of pretty pictures of trees and make a big fuss about seafood? A lot of silliness, if you ask me."

Marcie smiled to herself at the accuracy of the woman's comment.

"We do publish articles for tourists. But we also print a lot of stories about the history of the region. I think that's what we have here."

"A conspiracy is what we have," the woman said loudly. Her hands tightened on the arms of the chair as if squeezing someone's neck.

Marcie stared for a moment, finding it hard to believe that the sudden outburst had come from the prim woman who sat across from her.

"A conspiracy to commit murder. And the whole town was part of it."

Marcie smiled politely. "I'm sorry, I think you're ahead of me."

Miss Heller's eyes flashed. "Don't you want to write this down?"

Marcie dug her notebook out of her bag, reminding herself that she'd have to be more "reporterly" from now on.

"The whole thing started back in March of forty-four," Miss Heller began, sounding as if she was launching into a well-rehearsed story.

"What happened then?" Marcie asked. The woman gave her a glance that said, *Shut up and I'll tell you.*

"My brother Jake was driving home from The Lonesome Pine. He worked in Norm's Garage back then, and after work he liked to stop off for a beer." She paused to give Marcie a warning look that told her not to get the wrong idea. "But he never drank to excess," she added quickly.

"Did your brother live with your family at the time?"

"He lived right here with me, just the two of us. Mother and Father had recently passed away within a year of each other, but Jake and I decided to go right on living in the house, since we were used to it. No sense in changing just for the sake of change."

Marcie nodded, secretly thinking that sometimes that might be a pretty good reason. She took a surreptitious glance around the room at the time-warp furniture. Not changing for the sake of *anything* seemed to be Miss Heller's motto.

"So, as I was saying, my brother was driving back here from The Lonesome Pine at around seven o'clock.

He had to go through the center of town to get here. As he was passing the elementary school, a foolish boy shot out into the road on his bicycle—a completely irresponsible act. Jake slammed on the brakes. He always kept his car in tip-top condition, since he worked in a garage. But the boy pulled right out in front of him at the last minute. He was under Jake's wheels before my brother had time to react. There was nothing he could do. Walter Rickter, who used to own the general store, was standing nearby with a direct line of sight to the accident, and he told the police that there was no way Jake or anyone else could ever have stopped in time."

"What happened to the boy?"

"He died in the hospital up in Montpelier the next day."

"That's a shame," Marcie said.

The woman shook her head. "What's a shame is what happened afterward. People started talking among themselves. Saying that Jake was drunk and didn't even slow down until after the boy was run over. Before long people we'd known since we were born would hardly give us a nod. The owner of the garage told Jake he had to let him go because he was losing so much business. People were driving five miles out of town to take their trade to a different garage. Even at church people would be in a group talking, and when we'd walk over, they'd suddenly hush up like they were saying something about us that they wouldn't say to our faces. Miserable cowards. I wish they'd said what they had to say, so I could have given them a piece of my mind."

"What was the boy's name?"

Miss Heller paused and thought for a moment. "Joe

Campbell. He lived with his mother just a few blocks away from the school."

"Where was his father?"

"Away somewhere in the Army," the woman said quickly as if that were irrelevant to her story. "Anyway, things kept getting worse and worse. Jake had to drive ten miles each way to work at a different garage up north. It was really hard for him, but that wasn't enough for them."

"For whom?" Marcie asked.

"For the people in this town. Who else? It wasn't enough to shun us and get Jake fired." Miss Heller leaned toward her until Marcie thought the woman might fall off the chair onto the floor. "They wanted to kill Jake for something that had been an accident. And it got even worse when the boy's father died in the fighting in Europe. Some people claimed that that only happened because he'd lost the will to live once he heard that his son was dead. They made that all up, of course. Who could know something like that? But that got people blaming Jake for *his* death too."

"How did Jake come to be out in the Hayes barn?" Marcie asked.

The woman sank back in the chair and shook her head. "I was at a church meeting. Almost all the women in town were. I didn't even know that Jake wasn't home until I got back later that afternoon. Then I thought he had just gone for a ride or to have a drink with some friends."

"George Fuller and Matt Carter?"

"I didn't know who he was with," Miss Heller said; then she shrugged. "By that time, though, Jake didn't have many friends other than George and Matt. He'd gone through school with George, and Matt was just a year or two ahead of him. They used to get together a lot."

Marcie paused, not quite sure how to phrase the next question, then decided that the best approach was to be direct. "Why wasn't Jake in the military?"

The woman rocked forward in her chair so suddenly that Marcie jerked back.

"It wasn't that he didn't want to be, even though that vicious rumor got spread around pretty quick. He had a heart murmur, and they wouldn't take him. I told everyone that, but Jake was so big and healthy-looking, no one believed it. They didn't come right out and say we were lying, but even before the accident there were people that thought that he'd gotten special treatment from the draft board. But he'd always had that heart murmur, and the letter from the specialist in Boston that he went to told nothing but the truth. If they'd only known how disappointed Jake was when he got turned down, they would have realized that."

"What about George and Matt? Why weren't they drafted?"

"George ruined his knee playing football in high school. I'm not sure what was wrong with Matt."

"And you have no idea why the three of them were in the Hayes barn that afternoon?"

"The one thing I am sure of is that somebody in this town got them to go out there with the intention of murdering them. It was a plot to kill my brother because he accidentally ran over that boy."

"So you think somebody was taking justice into their own hands?"

"Justice!" Miss Heller shrieked, leaping to her feet. She covered the distance between them in an instant, grabbed Marcie by the arm, and pulled her to her feet. "If you think that was justice, young woman, you can get out of my house right now."

Marcie tried to apologize, but the woman put a firm hand on her back and forced her down the hall to the door.

"And I don't want you writing anything about what happened to my brother. You aren't fit to write about my darling. If I hear that you put a word of this on paper, I'll sue."

Marcie turned to apologize again but found that the door had been forcefully shut in her face.

I guess I still have to work on my interviewing technique, Marcie thought as she walked back to her car.

Chapter Six

Kevin was relieved. On the drive out to Fair Oaks, the assisted-living facility where Sarah Carter lived, he'd been dreading the thought of walking down green-tiled halls lined with people tied into wheelchairs, their eyes staring at him with hopelessness or incomprehension. Even more, he hated the thought of breathing in the pervasive smell of bodily functions inadequately concealed by deodorizers. That was his teenage memory of visiting people in a nursing home when he was in high school, part of a community outreach project meant to give young people an appreciation for the elderly. All it had ever given him was a fear of growing old and a hope that he would die quickly while in full possession of his faculties.

The lobby of Fair Oaks, however, reminded him of a nice hotel. The floor was tiled but in a nice mosaic pattern with muted colors. A plush rug filled the center of the room, with upholstered chairs arranged around a large-screen television. The people sitting there glanced up at him, aware of his presence. One woman even smiled. There was a man in a wheelchair, but he appeared alert and unrestrained. Kevin sniffed like a hunting dog and was happy not to detect any odors other than floor polish.

A pleasant staff person in a bright turquoise uniform took his name and directed him down a wide carpeted hallway to a door with a basket of artificial flowers hanging in the center. The woman who opened the door to greet him was a plump, rather jolly-looking woman wearing a pink sweatshirt and a pair of jeans. Mrs. Carter invited him in with a smile and directed him to a comfortable chair. She offered him some lemonade that she'd just made herself and put a plate of cookies on a table within easy reach.

As she proudly told him, her apartment consisted of a bedroom, a bathroom, and a sitting room, which Kevin could see had a sink, microwave, and small refrigerator along one wall. Although not large, it had the look of an upscale hotel suite, neatly arranged and nicely decorated. Kevin told her so.

Sarah Carter smiled. "The biggest mistake people make when they move into a place like this is that they want to keep all their furniture from where they were living before. It's understandable; we do become attached to things. But I only kept a few items like that vase, a couple of pillows, and that rocking chair in the corner. Other than that I gave everything away. I bought all new, smaller-sized furniture that would fit in better here."

"Downsizing must have been hard. You lived on a farm before, didn't you?"

"Yes. Phil and I lived in the large farmhouse until five years ago, when he died. Then our son and his family moved in there, and I shifted over to the small farmhouse."

"How did there come to be two houses on the property?" Kevin asked, sampling a cookie.

"Well, you see, two farms were combined. Phil and Matt's folks owned the first farm with the small house. When their father died back in 1940, their mom decided to move down to Hartford, Connecticut, to live with her unmarried sister. And she needed money to help her sister out with expenses. Matt was already out of school and had worked for a few years, so he scraped together some money and bought the farm from his mom. I don't imagine he paid much. Nobody had a lot around here back then. She made him promise to let Phil live there as long as he wanted."

She pushed the plate of cookies closer to Kevin. "Take more," she said with a motherly smile. "You look like you could use a little more weight on you."

"Was your husband still in school?" Kevin asked, reaching over to take a cookie with a jam center.

"He was a junior in high school when Matt took over."

"So the two boys were living on the family farm. How did they get the second farm?"

"Well, the Proctors had the farm right next to them. It was bigger and had this beautiful farmhouse that old Mr. Proctor had built. He and his wife had both died rather recently, and his son, Simon, was running it. He bought lots of new equipment and began using those scientific methods of agriculture that were just coming along at the time. They were like a picture-book family, Simon and Adele and the two little girls. I was only in my early teens myself, but I can still remember them driving up to church in their shiny Ford. They looked so happy." She paused. "Who knows what problems other families have, but at the time they seemed a lot better off than mine. However, it didn't last."

"What happened to them?"

"The war happened to them, like it did to a lot of other people. Simon was drafted. Only later did we find out that he had borrowed heavily to purchase all that new equipment. Then we had a really dry summer, and there was some kind of a sickness that spread through the live-stock. The final straw was when their barn burned down. They lost a lot of their remaining livestock and most of their equipment. Maybe if Simon had still been around, he would have been able to talk the bank out of foreclos-ing right away. But there was no one to help Adele. Adele Proctor was a fine mother, but she had no head for busi-ness."

"So Matt bought the farm?"

"On a bank foreclosure. Adele and the children went to live with her parents over in New Hampshire. We heard later that Simon was killed in combat. That's when the real trouble started, I suppose."

Kevin pushed the hair off his forehead and glanced up from his pad. "What trouble?"

"A rumor started that Matt had somehow gotten the

bank to foreclose quickly and not give Adele enough time to meet her loans. Some folks even suggested that he had started the barn fire. It didn't help that Matt and George Fuller, who worked at the bank, were friends. People figured that George had pulled some strings."

"But wasn't George Fuller only about Matt's age?" Kevin asked, recalling what he had learned from the obituaries of the murdered men. "He couldn't have had a very important position at the bank."

Sarah smiled gently as she recalled the past. "You wouldn't have thought so. In fact, everyone who knew George was a little surprised that he went into banking at all. He was this handsome, irresponsible, but terribly charming young man who had been a football hero before being hurt. The girls a little bit older than I were all taken with him. Banking really didn't seem to suit him. But with all the boys away in the war, there were lots of jobs for those still around, and one thing George liked was being able to dress up and not get his hands dirty with real work."

"But how did he get into a position with so much authority?" Kevin pressed.

"There was only George and old Mr. Williamson, the bank president, left to run the place. The rest of the employees were women. They were tellers, and back then that's right where they stayed. Only men got into management. Mr. Williamson was already slightly gaga, although the bank board didn't dare replace him until the war was over. That meant George had a lot more authority than would normally have been true."

Kevin paused and licked his lips. "Do you think there was any truth to the rumor about Matt and George's being involved in some sort of scam?"

Sarah looked across her sitting room, weighing the question. Kevin was surprised that there hadn't been a quick negative response.

"My husband always defended his brother and said that he wouldn't be involved in anything like that. But, to be honest, I was never so sure. Matt told Phil, who had just graduated from high school at the time, that he could go on living on the farm only as long as he earned his keep. Matt considered himself to be the owner of the farm and treated Phil as a kind of hired hand. I'm sure that their mother didn't expect it to be that way. She intended that at least the original farm would be a home for both of them, but Matt legally had the title to the farm, so that was that. Any man who would do that to his own brother, well . . ." The woman let the words fade away with significance.

"So these rumors about Matt began to spread?" Kevin asked to get back to the point.

"That's right. And so many people had this rosy picture of the Proctors that when everything ended tragically, what with the foreclosure and his death and all, they blamed Matt and George. It was as if the whole town turned against them. They were two young men not serving their country and taking advantage of those who were. I wasn't going out with Phil yet at the time, so I never knew how bad it was. But he told me all about it later. For that matter people even held it against Phil after he took over the farm, even though he put in a year in the Army right at the end of the war. After we got married, there were still some folks who wouldn't talk to me. Small towns have long memories."

"Why wasn't Matt in the military?" Kevin asked.

"He was hard of hearing. Oh, he covered it up pretty well, because he was good at reading lips, but it was genuine. It only came on as he got older, so a lot of people didn't believe he had trouble because he'd been fine as a boy. Phil developed the problem himself, but only when he got into his sixties."

"So Matt had a legitimate exemption?"

"Definitely. But it didn't matter. You can't imagine what it was like back in those days. Men turned down by their draft boards begged to be allowed to serve because they were so afraid of what the community would think of them. A few even committed suicide when they were rejected for service. After the way things were later with the draft protests about Vietnam, it's hard to realize how different it was during World War II."

Kevin nodded. "So Phil inherited when his brother was killed?"

"Matt didn't leave a will. He was so young, he probably didn't figure he needed one. So when he was murdered, his estate went to his mother. Phil bought the farm from her for a fair price and paid her back over years. If it wasn't for Phil, I don't know how she'd have gotten along, not on that little bit Matt gave her for the original farm. Phil was a good man."

Her eyes became teary, and she wiped at them with a tissue.

"I'm sure he was," Kevin said soothingly. "Did you

or your husband ever have any idea who might have killed Matt and the other two men that day?"

Sarah shrugged her ample shoulders. "Oh, later on when we were married and some people were nastier to us than others, we'd suspect them for a while. But we never had any evidence. The chief of police at the time, Jack McDermott, went around asking questions, but nothing ever came to light. It was a sleepy Sunday afternoon in July when it happened. Most of the women, including myself, were at a church meeting, and the men were who knows where. When I heard rumors at the meeting that Carter, Fuller, and Heller had been found hanged, I almost fainted because I thought at first that it was Phil. I was already sweet on him then, although we weren't really going out." She shook her head and smiled. "I'm afraid that's all I know."

Kevin nodded and closed his notebook. "Thanks for your time. I'll let you know how the story works out."

Sarah Carter nodded, clearly preoccupied with her thoughts. "The only idea I've ever had about the whole thing," she said slowly, "is that it couldn't have involved very many people."

"Why is that?" Kevin asked.

She smiled, showing the dimples in her chubby face. "Because people chatter so much in Doric that someone would have given it away."

There was a knock at the door.

"Come in," Sarah called out.

A heavyset man in his twenties entered. He walked over to Sarah and gave her a kiss on the cheek. He seemed surprised to see Kevin there.

"This is my grandson, Jason Andrews." She patted his hand affectionately. "He's my daughter Joan's boy. They live north of Montpelier, but he drove down today to take me out shopping."

The two men shook hands. Sarah explained why Kevin was there.

Her grandson gave a mock groan. "Not the hanging men again."

"Old news?" Kevin said.

Jason smiled. "We lived in Doric when I was a kid, so I went to school here. Every so often one of the kids would hear the story from a grandparent, and before long I'd be getting teased about having an uncle who was a ghost."

"How did that ghost thing get started?" Kevin asked, knowing that Marcie would want to know.

Sarah shook her head. "I never knew the whole story. The rumor was that Sel's mother, Felicia, was the first one to see them. And before long she had a couple of the women who worked out there spooked. People started saying that the spirits of the murdered men had come back seeking revenge. Sel's granddad started to have a tough time getting people to work on the farm after that. Like I said, during the war there were lots of job around, so folks could move on if they felt like it."

"It's funny, how quick people are to believe in supernatural stuff," Jason said. "I guess they just like being scared."

"I'm sure that's true," his grandmother replied. "But there was more to it than that this time. The idea that the ghosts of the dead men wanted vengeance got a lot of people nervous."

"Why's that?" Jason asked.

"Because they were already feeling guilty," his grandmother replied.

Chapter Seven

"You're involved in a murder case?" Amanda said, her voice rising dangerously.

Marcie could tell that Amanda was upset because she was repeating what Marcie had just told her.

"Well, only in a manner of speaking," she replied evasively.

Marcie was sitting on the bed in her room at the inn. She swung her feet up and stretched out. She tried to relax, knowing this was going to be a difficult conversation.

"What does that mean?" Amanda persisted.

"I don't think the police really believe I had anything to do with the hanging. In fact, the chief isn't even sure it was murder. He thinks it could have been suicide. They just want me to stay around in case they have any questions."

"Hanging? Who got hanged?"

"Seldon Hayes, the guy who was going to tell me

71

about the hanging men. At first the police thought that I was the last person to see him alive, other than the murderer of course, but then Kevin Murray told them that he had spoken to Sel on the phone after I left the farm. That kind of got me off the hook, so now I'm really more like a material witness."

"Who is Kevin Murray?" Amanda asked, with a clear note of impatience in her tone.

"Kevin Murray. He's a reporter for the *Courier.* That's a newspaper in Montpelier. He only a stringer, but his father owns the paper."

"How is he involved in all this?"

"I guess you could say that he was trying to beat me to the story. He planned to outbid us for Sel's information. But now that Sel is dead, we're sort of working together."

A deep sigh came from Amanda. "*What* are you working on *together*?" she asked.

Knowing that this was the part that Amanda really wouldn't like to hear, Marcie chose her words carefully.

"We're trying to reconstruct Sel's secret information about the original murders. We figured that way we could write the story from different angles and share it."

There was a long moment of silence that Marcie knew couldn't be good, because it meant that Amanda was carefully analyzing what she had just said. Marcie was sure that there was going to be trouble when Amanda asked, "Why was Hayes murdered?"

"That's what we're trying to find out."

"No, what you and your new friend are trying to find out is exactly what information he had that got him killed, but you already believe that he was murdered because of this story that he tried to sell to you. Isn't that true?"

"I suppose that's right."

"Which means that you are putting yourselves at risk by trying to discover what the murdered man knew. If the killer thinks that there's a chance of your finding out the truth about these hanging men, you'll be next on his hit list."

"What are the odds that the killer will find out?"

"Get real, Marcie. You're in a small town where people haven't got much to do but gossip. Everybody knows everything about everyone else. The word is probably already out all over town that the two of you are snooping around."

"I guess that's possible," Marcie admitted grudgingly. "But Kevin and I are working together. We'll look out for each other."

"That's nice," Amanda said.

Marcie wasn't sure whether she had detected any sarcasm in the word *nice*. Amanda was known to be a bit sarcastic at times if she thought you were doing something particularly stupid. Plus she'd been overworked since Greg went away, and that had happened right after she'd broken up with her boyfriend. All things considered, Marcie figured Amanda was entitled to be a little irritable.

"However, this person didn't hesitate to kill three people once before," Amanda continued, "so I don't think that knocking off the two of you will be a major roadblock to him."

"I don't think it's the same person," Marcie said, and

she went on to relate her theory about the unlikelihood of a geriatric murderer.

"Maybe so," Amanda replied, "but the new guy may not be any less ruthless."

Marcie couldn't deny the logic of Amanda's position, so she tried another avenue. "The thing is, I've already rescheduled all my appointments so I can spend three days here. I can't really change them all again. That wouldn't look very professional." Marcie knew that looking professional was important to Amanda.

"If you left right now and came back home, you could be here by tonight. That means you could help me around the office tomorrow, then go back out the next day."

Marcie groaned. "All that driving. Four hours back today. One day off, then four hours back out here again. That isn't very efficient."

"It is if it keeps you alive," Amanda snapped.

"But the chief of police ordered us to stay in town as material witnesses."

"I'll give him a call. The magazine will vouch for your return if needed."

Marcie felt her chest tighten. She wanted to respond angrily that Amanda shouldn't treat her like a child. And how was she going to learn anything about investigative reporting if she got pulled back home whenever there was any risk? But Marcie took a deep breath instead and reminded herself that Amanda wasn't a tyrant like her father but just someone who was looking out for her well-being. *Don't whine like a baby,* she told herself. *Try to explain your position the way a mature adult would.*

"I appreciate your concern for me," she said to Amanda, "and I understand that there is some risk. I've certainly learned that on the last two cases we covered together. But I think this could be a really great story. And although you don't know Kevin, he does seem trustworthy. I'll make sure that we stay together if anything the least bit dangerous comes up."

Amanda sighed again. "I don't know, Marcie. This whole thing sounds so shaky. It makes me really nervous."

Marcie gave a ragged laugh. "It makes me a little nervous too. But this is the first big story I've handled on my own. If I had to give it up now, I don't know if I'd have the nerve to try it again. You might have to keep me in the office as an editor and send someone else out to get the stories."

There was a long silence on the other end.

"Okay," Amanda finally said in a resigned tone, "but check in with me every evening. I want updates. And keep your cell phone with you. If you get into any trouble, give me a call right away."

"Will do," Marcie said. "And thanks."

"You're welcome. I just hope I don't come to regret my decision."

"When you read my story, you'll say it was the best decision you ever made."

"Let's hope so," Amanda replied, not sounding quite convinced.

After Marcie hung up, she sat staring across the room, feeling that in some way she had crossed a significant line in her life. She hadn't gotten up that morning planning to take any bold steps, but events had swept her along in a swift current that now had her involved in a murder investigation. Marcie hugged her legs to her chest. She had managed to sound confident with Amanda, but in truth she was frightened. As a little girl, whenever she told her father that she was scared, he would give her a disdainful look and say that fear was just your mind's way of telling you to try harder.

What a monster, she thought. Then she laughed out loud. *Wouldn't it be a hoot if it turned out that even my father was right once in a while?*

Chapter Eight

Marcie looked across the table at Kevin, who was staring at the lamb chop on his plate with the intensity that some men reserved for gazing into their girlfriend's eyes. She was having further doubts about his romantic potential. His initial appeal had been based on his reasonably good looks and his boyish demeanor. But the way he took it for granted that women wanted to mother him was beginning to worry her.

Some women might be looking for a man that they could mother and then dominate with a velvet fist, but Marcie was hoping to find a guy who would be an equal and responsible partner. She didn't want a tyrant like her father, but she also wasn't looking to become a female version of her father and single-handedly run the show.

One positive thing you could say for Kevin was that he seemed to be a good reporter. His plan on how to gather more information about the hanging men had worked well so far, and she had been very impressed with what he'd found out from Sarah Carter. Now they knew how both Matt Carter and Jake Heller fit into the equation.

"So Sarah's brother-in-law Matt was suspected of having used his connection with George Fuller to swindle a war widow," said Marcie.

Kevin paused long enough in his eating to nod.

"And I found out that Jacob Heller was despised for having run over the son of a soldier who was later killed."

"That was good work," Kevin said, after he had finished chewing his mouthful of food. "Too bad you couldn't have gotten in a few more questions before offending her."

"I did my best," Marcie said, irked at the criticism. "But I don't think she has any idea who was responsible for the murders, or she'd have given me her list of suspects right away. Heck, she'd have probably bumped them off herself by now. She hates the town in general but not anyone in particular."

"Sarah didn't have any candidates either," Kevin said, buttering his second roll. "All she said is that she thinks it couldn't have been a large group that was involved or something would have leaked out over the years. That sounds right to me, but it doesn't exactly narrow down our list of suspects."

"I still think that Sel's grandfather had to be involved somehow," Marcie said.

Kevin continued eating but flapped his right arm like a wounded chicken.

"I don't care if he was missing an arm," Marcie said. "He could have had help with that part of it. I can't believe that the Hayes farm was selected by accident, and it's just too much of a coincidence that no one was around the barn when the murders happened."

Kevin shrugged and cut off another piece of lamb chop.

"And think about it," Marcie said. "Sel told me that he had evidence as to who did the murders. Maybe he got that evidence from his grandfather. It could be that his grandfather kept it a secret while he was alive and passed it on to Sel when he died."

Kevin shook his head and swallowed. "My contact at The Lonesome Pine told me that Sel's grandfather died when Sel was seventeen. He fell down the stairs at home. That was fifty years ago."

"How does your contact happen to know what year the grandfather died?"

"When Sel had had a few drinks, he was inclined to feel sorry for himself. I guess he would go on about how his father was killed in the war, so he had to work on the farm with his granddad all the time he went to school. And then when his granddad died, he had to take over responsibility for whole place before he had a chance to have any fun."

"That's the third guy from Doric we've heard about who died in the war. That's a big sacrifice for one small town to make."

"It was a big war," Kevin replied. "The war to end all wars."

"I think that was the First World War."

Kevin shrugged. "That's what they say about every war."

"Do you know what year Sel's father was killed?" Marcie asked.

Kevin shook his head. "Anyway, my point is that if Sel got this evidence right after his grandfather died, why would he wait fifty years before going public? Whatever information he received, he got it recently."

Marcie sat quietly for several minutes mulling over the case, while Kevin scooped up the last of his mashed potatoes.

"Okay," she finally said. "I don't know where Sel's evidence came from, but he sure spoke as if he had something that was pretty solid."

Kevin paused and pointed his fork at her. "But he never showed you any real proof. It could have just been talk. He might have been trying to con both of us."

"I think we can safely assume that if he didn't have any real proof, he'd be sitting in The Lonesome Pine hoisting some brews tonight instead of cooling on a slab in Montpelier. Somehow he convinced his killer that he was a threat. I figure that took some pretty solid evidence."

Kevin put down his knife and fork. "Good point."

"And you know what that means?" Marcie asked with the confidence of someone who already has a ready answer.

Kevin thought for a moment, then asked, "What?"

"It means that Sel probably had something tangible. Some kind of physical proof that after all this time would indicate who killed those men. And where do you think he would have kept something like that?"

"Unless he had a safe deposit box, he probably kept it right at the farm," Kevin said.

Marcie nodded, her eyes shining. "That means we've got to get access to the farm."

"I don't think the chief is going to let us go snooping around out there."

"Well, we certainly aren't going to tell him that's why we want to go there."

"Then what *are* we going to tell him?"

Marcie opened her mouth to speak, when Kevin looked toward the doorway and began to frantically roll his eyes.

"What's the matter with—"

"I thought I might find the two of you here."

Chief Roylston loomed over them. His eyebrows were pressed together in a straight line forming a partial equator around the globe of his hairless head.

"Hi, Chief," Marcie said brightly.

"I want to talk to both of you."

"Pull up a chair," Kevin said.

"We're not quite done. . . ." Marcie began.

"These two will be back in a few minutes," the chief said to the passing waitress. "Let's go over to the lobby, where it will be quieter."

Since the dining room was no more crowded than the other night, Marcie suspected that the chief wanted it to be exceptionally quiet when he spoke with them. She didn't think that was a good sign.

Herding them in front of him like a couple of stray sheep, the chief marched them out of the dining room, past the reception desk, and into the lobby. He kept them going until they were as far away as possible from other people, then motioned for them to sit next to each other on a love seat, while he positioned himself directly across from them.

"What the hell do you two think you're doing?"

"Excuse me?" Marcie asked, her eyes wide with innocense.

"Did you really think that you could go around town talking to people about Sel's murder without my hearing about it?" He stared hard at Kevin. "You're not the only one with contacts."

Marcie realized that Amanda was absolutely right about how fast news traveled in a small town.

"You're interfering with an ongoing police investigation," Roylston continued. "That's a crime."

"We aren't talking to people about Sel's murder," Marcie said.

One of the chief's eyebrows became a sarcastic question mark. "Then what are you doing?"

"We're interviewing people about the men who were murdered on the Hayes farm over sixty years ago. Is that an ongoing investigation?"

"Of course not," Roylston snapped; then he looked puzzled for a moment, as if not certain whether an open murder investigation six decades old could be considered ongoing or not. A smile of triumph appeared on his face. "We all know that if Sel was murdered, then it could be connected to the hanging men," he said. "So by digging into one, you're digging into the other."

"They *could* be connected," Marcie agreed. "But they might not be. I don't think you should be accusing us of committing a crime without more evidence than that."

The chief pursed his lips and sat back in the chair. "Look, I understand that you two are on to a story here. Now, it may be a story about the past, but there's a murderer out there right now who may well see it as directly connected to a killing that is only about twenty-four hours old. If that turns out to be the case, your poking around could turn out to be dangerous."

Marcie squirmed nervously in the love seat, bumping hips with Kevin. She knew what the chief said was true, but to give up now, when they were so close to possibly finding the answer to the murder of the hanging men, would be a huge disappointment. After all of her brave talk to Amanda, she had to come back with something worth writing about.

"We'll be okay, Chief," Kevin said. "We'll keep an eye on each other."

Roylston shook his head. "That might not be enough protection if you keep going around town asking questions, so I'm taking back my request that you not leave Doric. In fact, I'm asking that you do leave—and as soon as possible."

"I don't think you can force us to leave town," Kevin said. "We haven't committed any crime."

"Stay if you want; it's only a request," the chief said sharply. "I'm just trying to keep the two of you alive."

"Is that all there is to it?" Kevin asked. "Or are you also interested in seeing that the full story about the hanging men remains hidden, because if it got out, it might be embarrassing to the town?"

A guilty expression quickly passed over the chief's face, telling Marcie there was some truth in Kevin's accusation. Then his face grew red as he struggled to get a handle on his temper.

"I'm only looking out for your well-being, son, no matter what you think," he replied, getting ready to stand.

"Chief, I think we might be able to come up with a compromise on this," Marcie said in her most soothing voice.

Roylston reluctantly settled back down in his chair and looked at her doubtfully.

"I've pretty much got all the information I need for my story, at least until your investigation brings more to light. I'm just going to do a piece on what I've found out up to now and sort of allude to what might be discovered in the future. What I really need, however, are some pictures of the Hayes farm." Marcie smiled disarmingly. "Although I hate to admit it, a magazine sells more based on its photography than on the written word. Would you give me permission to go to the farm and take a few photos?"

The chief regarded her carefully. "After you got your pictures, you'd leave town?"

Marcie nodded.

"What about you?" the chief said to Kevin.

Kevin looked puzzled at Marcie's suggested compromise, and for a moment she thought that he might refuse to go along. Then he smiled slightly, and she could see that he had figured out her plan.

"I guess that would be fine with me too, Chief," he said slowly. "Montpelier isn't very far away. I can always come back if my sources tell me that you've discovered anything new."

The chief scowled at the mention of "sources" but then nodded, apparently pleased that they had finally seen the light and were going to leave town.

"A few pictures around the farmyard is all you need?"

Marcie shook her head. "Indoor shots are always more useful. And we'd certainly need several photos of the infamous beam."

"Well, it's all right with me, but you'll have to check with Steve McDermott. He's the lawyer who's handling Sel's estate. I'll give him a call and let him know what you want to do. He'll get in touch with you."

"Is that Steve McDermott the state representative?" Kevin asked.

The chief nodded.

"Who are Sel's heirs?" Kevin asked.

"As far as I know, he didn't have any family left, at least not around here." The chief gave Kevin a small smile. "Just to head you off at the pass, I doubt that anyone would have killed him to get that farm. And Sel probably didn't have much else to his name."

"I'll make a note to check with McDermott just to be sure," Kevin said, pulling out his pad.

"And make a note right next to it to leave town when you're done at the farm," the chief added.

"Did you find out any more from the medical examiner about Sel's death?" Kevin asked, unfazed.

The chief paused as if considering whether to answer. "Sel did have a broken neck."

"That means he was thrown from the hayloft, so it couldn't have been suicide," said Kevin.

"He could have jumped," the chief said.

"I thought you found a ladder under the rope. That would suggest that he was standing," Marcie said.

"Maybe he tried it one way, and it didn't work. So he went up into the hayloft to make sure he got it right."

"Pretty persistent," Marcie added dryly.

"Some suicides are."

"Or maybe someone tried to make it look like a suicide," Kevin added.

The chief got to his feet and looked down on Kevin and Marcie as if they were troublesome students that he suspected would get up to mischief as soon as he turned his back.

"So we have a deal. You take your pictures and then leave me alone to conduct my investigation."

"And you'll let us know if anything new turns up," Marcie said.

"Of course."

"Then you've got a deal," Marcie said, and Kevin added his agreement.

The chief gave them a long look as if trying to detect any subterfuge; then he nodded and left.

"Do you really think he'll tell us if he finds out anything new?" Marcie asked softly, twisting around so she faced Kevin on the love seat.

"When pigs fly, to coin a phrase," Kevin said, pushing the hair off his forehead. "And I don't think the chief would be too disappointed if nothing new turned up. Did you see the expression on his face when I accused him of being more interested in protecting the town than in finding the truth?"

Marcie nodded. "The idea I'm getting from the folks we've talked to so far is that nobody looked really closely into those murders at the time they happened because the victims were unpopular. Most people were sort of caught up in the wartime hysteria and figured that those guys were a bunch of sneaky draft dodgers who got what they deserved. Only their families felt differently."

"And it wouldn't be real pretty to have that story get out, even today. 'The Town That Served As Judge and Jury.' I can see the front page headline in the *Courier* already." A dreamy expression came over Kevin's face. "I'll bet some national publications would pick up on a story like that."

"But it would be an even better story if we could also reveal who did the killings," Marcie added.

"Yeah. By the way, it took me a minute to catch on, but it was brilliant how you came up with a way for us to get onto the Hayes farm. Now we'll be able to hunt around and see if Sel hid any evidence about the killer's identity."

"Unless the chief is there, watching our every move," Marcie pointed out.

"Even if he is, I bet one of us will have a chance to get alone long enough to unlock a window, so we could return for an unauthorized visit in the evening."

The thought of prowling around the Hayes farm in the middle of the night sent a chill up Marcie's spine. She looked across the empty lobby to the warm glow coming from the dining room.

"Why don't we go back to our table and have some dessert?"

Kevin smiled and unfolded his lanky frame from the love seat.

"Great. I thought you'd never ask."

Marcie sat on her bed. She'd just popped a flash drive into her laptop that contained most of the articles for the next issue of *Roaming New England*. If she was going to be away from the office, the least she could do was catch up on some of the editing. That way they wouldn't have fallen too far behind by the time she returned.

Now that the chief had given her permission to leave town, she was feeling a bit guilty about hanging around for even one more day to take the photos of the farm, while Amanda was slaving away back at the office. Despite what she had told Roylston, it was very questionable whether the magazine would even publish the story, given the direction it was taking. *Roaming New England* wasn't really into investigative journalism. Scenery, leisure activities, and the paranormal pretty much covered the magazine's range of interests. It was hard to see how the hanging men would fit in. The first two categories were certainly out: no pleasant scenery or recreational fun in this story. And the paranormal angle needed more investigating. Marcie decided to think a bit more the next day about how to research the ghost stories Sel had referred to. She wondered what had happened to Sel's mother, Felicia Hayes. According to what Sarah Carter had told Kevin, she was the first one to see the ghosts of the hanging men.

Marcie hoped she could combine the ghost story with some new information about the murders. Heller, Fuller, and Carter might not have been very nice men, Marcie concluded, but they hadn't deserved to have their deaths be so easily dismissed. Maybe she could do something to see that they finally got the justice they deserved.

Chapter Nine

"*McDermott, McDermott and McDermott,*" Kevin read aloud. "You'd think one *McDermott* would be enough."

The large white sign with green lettering was in the center of the gracious front lawn of the two-story house that occupied a corner lot near the center of town.

"I guess they want you to know that they've been around for a while. Probably gives their clients a sense of security," Marcie said.

Kevin nodded. "Reassures them that somebody will actually show up for their bail hearing."

Chief Roylston had called the inn shortly after breakfast the next morning to tell Marcie that Steve McDermott had no objection to their visiting the farm, and they could stop by the lawyer's office anytime after nine to get the key to the house. She and Kevin had decided to pick up the key right away and go directly to the farm to conduct a search before anyone in authority had time to change his mind.

"Do you think Steve McDermott is related to the police chief who investigated the original hangings?" Marcie asked as they walked up the steps and across the front porch.

"That might have been Steve's great-grandfather. I've met Steve a couple of times around Montpelier when the legislature is in session. He's only in his early thirties."

As they walked inside, a young woman behind a glass window slid the panel back and asked whom they were there to see. She told them to sit across the way in the waiting room for a moment. They barely had time to appreciate the comfort of the deep leather chairs, when a slender, older woman in a business suit walked into the room.

"Ms. Ducasse, Mr. Murray, Attorney McDermott will see you now."

They followed her down a wide hallway with a highly polished wood floor.

"We must be on our way to see the boss. I guess they're not just going to toss us the key like it's a cheap rental," Kevin whispered.

"I thought this was too good to be true. I bet McDermott is going to give us the third degree. Let's just hope we get the key after all," Marcie whispered back nervously.

She didn't like lawyers or doctors. People who had access to specialized knowledge that could have a substantial impact on her life made Marcie feel out of control.

She wanted to make her own decisions and didn't like having to rely on experts.

The woman opened the door and walked into a spacious office, which held several more chairs and a desk with a large computer screen. Several doors led off of this central hub. She opened one of them and stepped to the side.

By the time Marcie and Kevin went through the doorway, the man who had been sitting behind the desk had come halfway across the room to greet them.

"Kevin, good to see you again," Steve McDermott said, shaking the other man's hand. "How's your father?"

Kevin mumbled a vague reply to the question and introduced Marcie. McDermott shook her hand with surprising gentleness, then motioned both of them into chairs. Instead of going around behind his desk to sit in his impressive office chair, he pulled over a chair from a corner and placed it so they were sitting in an informal circle. He immediately began reminiscing about the last time he and Kevin had seen each other in a downtown restaurant.

Just some friends getting together, Marcie thought. McDermott seemed pretty genuine for a politician. He was good-looking, but not so handsome that other men would doubt his mental abilities. His face broke into an easy smile as he chatted with Kevin, and he seemed very much at ease, exuding a kind of quiet confidence. There was none of the need to overwhelm or impress that Marcie had seen in the few public figures she'd met. For that matter, even Kevin seemed more poised and polished. Gone was the nervous pushing back of the hair and the boyish grin, and Marcie wondered whether his awkward-ness only showed when he was around women.

McDermott turned his attention to Marcie and asked her some questions about *Roaming New England* and her work there. He seemed pleased that there was such a magazine and suggested a couple of areas of Vermont that might be of particular interest for articles. Marcie had the feeling that he was really paying attention to what she had to say. Finally he cleared his throat and smiled as a sort of punctuation point, and Marcie could tell that they were about to get down to the real business at hand.

"Well, I guess it's time for me to sound like a lawyer," McDermott said with an apologetic smile. "Chief Royl-ston tells me that you would like to have access to the Hayes farm. I don't have any problem with that, but as the executor of Mr. Hayes' estate, I have to formally ask what your purpose would be in going onto the premises." He smiled sadly at even having to raise the point.

Marcie launched into her explanation of the "Weird Happenings" column and how she was writing a piece for it on the original hangings and the supernatural events that had supposedly taken place later at the farm. She said that she'd really like to get some pictures of the inside and outside of the barn and a few photos of the farmhouse.

"So you're not writing about my client's death?" asked McDermott.

"His death would be mentioned at the end because it ties in with the events of sixty years ago. But I would just end with a line like, 'Will a fourth ghost now be appear-ing in the barn at the Hayes farm?'"

McDermott nodded and appeared to take her seriously,

unlike many others who thought that writing about the supernatural was silly.

"And do you plan to speculate in the article about who might have murdered the three men?" he asked. "The chief mentioned to me that Sel thought he had some new information about that."

She shook her head. "We have no idea what that information might have been, if it existed at all. I plan to talk a bit about the men's backgrounds and what happened to them, but nothing beyond that." *Unless I find out what Sel knew,* she added to herself.

McDermott turned to Kevin. "And what do you plan to write for the *Courier*?"

"We've already run a story giving the facts of Sel's death. I'm planning to write a longer piece just laying out what the police know about the murders sixty year ago and then summarizing the state of the current investigation."

"Which isn't very promising, from what I hear," McDermott said sadly.

"Did you know Sel Hayes very well?" Kevin asked.

The lawyer shook his head. "My great-grandfather knew him the best. That was back when Sel was a boy. The rest of us all knew him casually from around town. He was kind of a local character."

"Was your great-grandfather the chief of police in the nineteen-forties?" asked Marcie.

"That's right. He investigated the original murders on the farm." McDermott's face tightened. "Unfortunately, he didn't make much progress. The newspapers all over the region, even as far away as New York and Boston, had a field day with it. They kept suggesting that only an incompetent or corrupt police chief would be unable to discover who killed three men in a small Vermont town. What they didn't understand was how strongly disliked these men were and how completely the town closed ranks to protect whoever had killed them."

"Your great-grandfather never had any suspicions?" asked Kevin.

"I don't know. He never spoke much about the case as far as I've heard. He retired from the chief's job a couple of years after the killings. He was only in his midfifties, but he returned to farming. His son, Luke, my grandfather, had just come back to town after finishing his studies and established this firm. My great-grandfather used that as an excuse to leave the police, claiming that there might be a conflict of interest. No one ever really believed that. It was the case of the hanging men that broke him."

"I'm sure not knowing what happened haunted him for the rest of his life," Marcie said. "That's how I would feel, anyway."

McDermott nodded. "You're exactly right. No matter what good things took place after that in his life, I think the hanging men were always on his mind. It followed him like a dark cloud. That's why I had hoped, when I heard that Sel was talking around town about having new information, that this whole issue could be laid to rest once and for all. But I guess now that will never happen."

"Who are the other McDermotts on your sign?" Marcie asked.

The man's face brightened. "My father joined

Granddad in the early seventies. And now . . ." He gestured at the office to show that he was continuing the family tradition. "Actually, I'm the only one still active in the practice. My granddad passed away, and my father recently retired to Florida. He said that as much as he enjoyed the practice of law, he was thoroughly sick of the long, cold Vermont winters."

Steve McDermott walked over to his desk and came back with a key. He handed it to Marcie. "I've taken a look around, and there's certainly nothing of much value lying about. But be sure to lock up the house when you leave. I'll need the keys back as soon as possible."

"We'll go out there right now," Marcie said.

"Can you tell me who Sel left his estate to? He didn't have any family, did he?" Kevin asked.

McDermott shook his head. "He was married for almost twenty years, but they never had any children. His wife died of cancer back in the late eighties. It was after her death that poor Sel began to get really strange. He went on disability from his factory job and began hanging around the farm, drinking more than was good for him. When he came to see me about making up his will, I was curious about how he was going to dispose of his assets, since he had no family."

"What did he decide?" Kevin asked.

McDermott paused. "I guess there's no harm in telling you. I've already notified his heirs informally by phone, and it will be public knowledge in a few weeks when we go to probate. He left the farm equally to Sarah Carter and Rachel Heller. I asked him why he picked them, and he said that he'd always felt guilty about what happened on the farm that day. They'd gone through a lot because of it but stayed in town, just like he had. He figured they deserved to be rewarded."

"They didn't know about this inheritance before-hand, did they?" Marcie asked, not that she could see two elderly women stringing up Sel to get the farm.

"Not to my knowledge. I don't think Sel had any intention of telling them."

"Is the farm worth much?" asked Kevin.

"There's about a hundred and fifty acres left. It would depend on whether a developer came along and wanted to use it for something."

"Did he have any other assets? Was there a safe deposit box, bank accounts, or anything like that?" Kevin asked.

McDermott shook his head, then got to his feet, indicating that the meeting was over. "Just return the key to the receptionist when you're finished. It's been great to see you again, Kevin. Give my best to your father." He turned to Marcie and smiled. "Please send me a copy of your story when it's published. As you can imagine, this is an episode that means a lot to me and to my family."

"I certainly will," Marcie said, thinking that this was a man she'd like to see again.

As they left the building, Kevin pumped a fist in triumph. "We've got the key. We can look around the farm to our heart's content."

Marcie nodded but was more subdued.

"What's the matter?"

"Nothing. I just have a feeling that whoever murdered Sel has already looked around the place pretty carefully.

They've either found the evidence, or it's going to be impossible to find."

Kevin patted her on the back. "Cheer up, fair lady. There are two of us. That means there are two heads, and you know what they say about that."

Two heads, two nooses, Marcie thought grimly.

"So what did you think of Steve McDermott?" Kevin asked.

"He seems like a nice, smart guy."

Kevin frowned. "Remember, he's a politician. He's bound to be good at hiding what he's really like."

Marcie gave him a sidelong glance and wondered whether Kevin was jealous because McDermott had showed an interest in what she had to say.

"I'll keep that in mind," she replied, smiling to herself.

The drive out to the Hayes farm was more pleasant for Marcie than the first time she had made the trip. At least she wasn't alone, and Kevin kept her amused with a long story about how he had managed to liberate the SUV they were using from the *Courier*'s vehicle pool. Marcie thought that having the name of the paper stenciled on both sides made it somewhat less than stylish, but she liked riding a bit higher. The SUV also absorbed the bumps in the gravel road better than her old sedan had. The scraping of the branches along the sides of this wider vehicle, however, made her cringe as they rode down the lane to the farm.

"Aren't you afraid someone will complain if you get this thing all scratched up?" she finally asked, after a particularly vicious branch ran along its side.

"I don't have a car of my own, so what can I do?" Kevin replied.

You could go out and buy one, thought Marcie, *instead of living off your parents.* Then she chided herself for being uncharitable. After all, her relationship with her own family was hardly ideal.

"Anyway, the motor pool expects a certain amount of wear and tear."

"I hope for your sake they have a generous policy."

Kevin just smiled.

"I know. When you're the son of the owner, nobody complains," Marcie said.

Kevin smiled again.

When they finally reached the farmyard, Kevin got out of the vehicle and stood for a moment looking around.

"I hadn't quite imagined from your description exactly how run-down this place is. It looks abandoned." He studied the barn. "So that's the scene of the crime."

"All the crimes," Marcie corrected. She reached into the canvas bag she had brought and got out two flashlights. She handed one to Kevin. "We'll certainly need these for the barn. I'm hoping that the farmhouse has working electricity."

"Where should we start?" Kevin asked, still sounding amazed by the state of disrepair.

"Let's begin with the house. If I were going to hide something, I think that would be my first choice."

They walked across the yard and up the two steps to the porch. The steps were bowed in the middle. Marcie could imagine the parade of feet that had marched up to the porch over the years. The nails had come out on one end of the top step, giving it a kind of bouncy quality, as if it were urging them to move along quickly. Kevin pulled back the ancient screen door, which emitted the sharp metal-on-metal squeal that Marcie remembered from her meeting with Sel. To her surprise, however, the screen door concealed what appeared to be a brand new vinyl front door with a deadbolt lock.

Kevin laughed. "Well, this certainly isn't original equipment. Maybe the first door finally rotted away, and he had to replace it."

"Or else Sel decided that he wanted to keep the place more secure."

The newness of the house ended with the door. Formerly white curtains, now sooty with dirt and half-rotten, kept the front room in shadows. Kevin hit a switch, and a ceiling light with dead bugs in its globe cast a yellowish glow over what appeared to be a dining room with a heavy pine table filling the center. Two matching chairs faced each other at one end of the table. Four other chairs were arranged randomly along the walls. The only other furniture was a huge china closet that occupied one corner. It appeared to be full of objects, although the dust and smudges on the glass made it almost impossible to see clearly what was inside.

Marcie pulled open the china closet door. There was a complete set of formal china with a gold leaf pattern. A number of large serving bowls and platters filled up the center shelves. On the bottom were small statuettes of children and animals that reminded her of the ones her mother had inherited from her grandmother. The dining room furniture had probably been nice fifty years ago when it was purchased, Marcie thought, but scratches and digs of various sorts had left it looking worn and tired. And the table's surface showed the stains of various spills.

On the left a narrow stairway led to the second floor. To the right was a room that appeared to be a living room. A carpet covered the wood floor, and a large, old television stood almost in the middle of the room. Its odd placement made sense when Marcie saw that it put the screen right in line with a red velour recliner. The sag in the cushions and numerous cigarette burns on the arms indicated that this had been Sel's favorite spot. Next to the chair a table with a marble top held a reading lamp and an ashtray overflowing with butts. A battered sofa and an equally worn upholstered chair were lined up right next to it. That had probably given Sel the choice of several seats for his viewing pleasure. In the far corner was a metal office desk.

"His decorating style was certainly eclectic," said Kevin. "You can tell no woman lived here."

"At least not recently," Marcie said. "I suspect his wife or mother bought that dining room furniture, and the sofa and chair look like the remnants of a living room set."

Kevin eyed the desk. "That seems promising." He walked across the room and pulled open the middle drawer. "Not locked," he said. "Maybe not so promising after all. Sel would have kept it locked if it contained anything important."

"You can open one of those with a paper clip."

Kevin raised an eyebrow.

"That's the kind of office furniture they use in the military. My father showed me how to do it. Sel might have kept it locked, but the killer or the police could have opened it even without the key."

"Guess I'll take a look through it, anyway," Kevin said, rolling out the metal desk chair and taking a seat.

Marcie nodded. "I'll check out the kitchen."

That room had once been painted a bright yellow. Marcie could imagine Sel's wife when she first moved in as a new bride asking to have a nice, cheerful kitchen and being well satisfied with the sunflower yellow color. Years of dirt had turned it to a shade closer to mustard. The white stove showed the results of many meals that Sel had let splatter over onto various surfaces, and the kitchen cabinets were thick with grease. Fortunately, however, there weren't many of them, and Marcie had emptied them all out, checking for any hidden materials, by the time Kevin entered the room holding a metal box about the size and depth of a large phone book.

"I think we're out of luck," he announced, holding the box out in front of him as if he were begging for coins.

Marcie took it from him.

"Look at the label on the top."

She flipped the box closed. A handwritten label, taped in place, read: *Quentin Hayes.*

"Was that Sel's grandfather's name?" Marcie asked, realizing that she had never heard him referred to by name before.

Kevin nodded.

"You found it empty, I take it," Marcie said.

"Unlocked and empty. I'll bet the killer took whatever was in there. I was thinking about what you said earlier. Who else but Sel's grandfather would have been able to tell him anything about the murders? Heck, his grandfather probably was in on it."

"But when I came up with that theory, you made a good point. Sel's grandfather has been dead for fifty years. Why would Sel only now be finding out who killed those men?"

"Maybe I have it wrong, and he knew all along but only recently needed money and decided to blackmail the killer."

Marcie frowned. "I don't think Sel's life has ever been easy. And the way he tried to hit me up for money, I think he'd have been out there hustling as soon as he got the information."

"Well, anyway, it looks like the evidence is gone now. I guess Sel's killer got it, whatever it was." Kevin flipped the box closed. "We may as well wrap it up."

"Since we're here, let's not stop until we're sure," Marcie said. "Leaving valuable information in a cheap metal box with a label on it seems a bit simpleminded even for Sel. I think we should keep looking just in case."

"Okay," Kevin said doubtfully. "I'll poke around in the living room some more."

Marcie went through the canisters on the kitchen counter. All were empty except the one containing sugar. She spooned through it and found nothing. The refrigerator had been emptied and turned off. Nothing was hidden among the meager supply of pots and pans. A full bathroom was off the kitchen. She had learned out west that when indoor plumbing got started, the water first came into the kitchen, so when bathrooms replaced outhouses, they were often installed near the kitchen, where there was a water supply. This bathroom had been remodeled sometime in the sixties. The sink and tub were avocado green. A quick check of the toilet tank, as she had seen people do on television, revealed nothing but a rusty mechanism.

A short hall off the kitchen ended at the back door. That was a new one as well, with a solid lock. Sel was definitely up to something, Marcie thought. Another door off the back hallway led down to the basement. The cellar was shallow—Marcie's head barely cleared the floor joists. It was also pretty dank. The floor was made of packed dirt with the beams resting on large flat stones that had been pounded into the earth, and the walls were constructed of smaller stones barely held in place with crumbling mortar. She peered into all the corners, using her flashlight, but found nothing but spider webs and an old furnace.

Kevin was just returning the drawers to the desk as she came into the living room.

"Anything interesting?" Marcie asked.

He shook his head. "McDermott probably has all the financial records, such as they were, so I can't tell if Sel was paying his bills on time or not. He'd only have had utilities, phone, and taxes. Since the phone and lights still work, I'd guess he was up to date. There's no checkbook or bank statements, so we can't find out if there were any recent sizeable deposits that would indicate that he was blackmailing someone."

"Let's move along to the next floor," Marcie said.

They went back to the front room and up the narrow stairway to the second floor. One door stood open; the other was closed. The open door led into a bedroom facing toward the farmyard and was obviously Sel's. There was an unmade bed, a shirt draped over a chair, and several pairs of shoes scattered about the floor. Marcie left Kevin to search there and opened the closed door across the hall. She found a back bedroom looking out in the direction of the meadows behind the house. That room contained only a bed, simply but neatly made up with a country-style quilt, a chest of drawers, a bedside table, and a single chair. A braided rug occupied the center of the room. A thick, even layer of dust covered the surfaces as if the room was rarely entered and never cleaned.

"A guest room?" Kevin asked from the doorway.

"I doubt Sel ever had guests. Maybe it was his wife's bedroom."

"They didn't sleep together?" Kevin asked, then blushed.

"Maybe not. Or maybe she was sick for quite a while before she died and used this room." Marcie opened a drawer in the chest, uneasily anticipating that she would find it filled with the dead woman's clothes. But all the drawers were empty. A quick search showed the same to be true of the entire room.

"I guess he got rid of his wife's things, then just closed the door and left the room," Marcie said.

"Closing the door on painful memories."

Marcie glanced at Kevin, a little surprised at his sensitivity.

"Possibly. Or maybe Sel handled problems by just forgetting about them and moving on."

They went back out into the hall.

"Anything in there?" Marcie asked, indicating Sel's bedroom.

Kevin shook his head. "The chest had two empty drawers. The third held underwear. A few shirts and pants in the closet, nothing under the bed or in the night-stand, except for a flashlight that didn't work.

At the end of the hall was another door, which revealed a stairway leading up into the attic.

Kevin switched on the stairway light and started up. "According to those television antique shows, people are always finding that their attics are filled with price-less heirlooms."

"I'd be happy with a piece of paper saying who-dunit," Marcie replied.

To their surprise, the attic wasn't a simple storage area. It had been finished off as a rather large bedroom that ran from one side of the house to the other. The slope of the roof made the room narrow and long.

"I wonder why they needed another bedroom," Kevin wondered.

Marcie looked around at the old furniture.

"You know, I'll bet this was where Sel's grandfather and grandmother slept back in the old days. Probably Sel's father and mother had that downstairs front bed-room, and when Sel was a boy, he slept in the back."

Marcie paused for a moment. "I wonder what happened to them all."

"Who do you mean?"

"Well, we know that Sel's father died in the war, and his grandfather fell down the stairs." Marcie looked behind her at the attic stairs as if expecting to see a body. "But what happened to the women: his mother and grandmother?"

"I'm sure somebody around town will know. I'll check."

"With your contact."

Kevin smiled. "Bartenders know all, and what they don't know, they can find out. What I've been thinking is that it must have been a long walk at night from here down to the one bathroom behind the kitchen."

"People were tougher back then," Marcie said. "I wonder if that's how the grandfather fell, going down to the bathroom one night."

Kevin walked across the room to where a section of wall between two studs had been removed. He glanced up at the white ceiling that was stained the color of tea.

"Looks like Sel had a leak in the roof, and it damaged this wall. The plaster must have started to come down. I guess Sel pulled it out and was going to repair it." Kevin used his flashlight to peer through the gap. "Hey, I see a box of stuff."

Kevin turned sideways and slipped through the opening. Marcie directed her flashlight into the space. Kevin, who was bent almost double to avoid banging his head on the roof trusses, was pushing a wide box back toward the opening.

"That's too large to fit," Marcie said. "Unload it under there and hand any stuff that looks like it might be important out to me."

She soon had a photograph album, ledger books labeled from 1921 to 1939 filled with farm accounts, and a small porcelain doll in a mildewed white dress arrayed around her on the floor. A brief glance through the album showed that it had belonged to Sel's grandfather. The picture at the front was of him as a skinny little boy in a sailor suit sitting on a stoop in what looked like an urban alley. His serious expression said that this was someone who had already seen too much of the world. The last picture was of the grandfather standing next to a young man in a military uniform and was dated 1942.

"I'll bet Quentin's son took over the farm in thirty-nine—that's when the ledgers end—then went to war in forty-two and never came back," Marcie said, as Kevin crawled out from under the eaves and announced that the rest of the stuff in the box was just old clothes. She looked down at the books spread out around her on the floor. "You know, what we have here is a record of the early business and personal life of Sel's grandfather."

"Right," Kevin said, leafing through the ledgers. "But it ends too soon. So far I haven't come across anything that looks like it would contain information about the murders." He took the photo album, turned it upside down, and gave it a shake. A card fell out.

"What's that?" Marcie asked.

Kevin picked it up. "It's one of those memorial cards they give out at funeral parlors. It answers one of the questions you asked earlier. It says that Rebecca Hayes, wife of Quentin Hayes, died in July of 1940."

Marcie pulled her legs up to her chest and sat still on the floor for a moment. "That means that at the time the men were hanged, there were only three people living in the house: Sel, his mother, and his grandfather."

Kevin stared down the long room, a pensive expression on his face.

"What are you thinking?" Marcie asked.

"I'm thinking about the room arrangement. You said that the front room downstairs probably was used by Sel's father and mother, and the back room was used by him. That means this attic was most likely the grandfather and grandmother's."

"That's what I figured."

"So I wonder how this box of stuff ended up back there behind a wall."

"What are you getting at?" Marcie asked.

"Well, if Sel had finished this room off later, I suppose he might have accidentally left granddad's memorabilia under the eaves. But if, as you say, this room was completed while the grandfather was still alive . . ."

"Then it was put there on purpose by Quentin Hayes," Marcie concluded.

"Right. Back then a farmer wouldn't have hired someone to do a construction job like this. He'd probably have done it himself."

"So Quentin Hayes walled up his own stuff," Marcie said. Then she shook her head. "Won't work."

"Why not?" Kevin asked.

"Because if the grandparents were already using this room, how did the grandmother's funeral notice get behind the wall?"

"Okay, how about this? The grandmother dies in 1940. The men are hanged in forty-four. At some point after that Quentin decides he wants to hide something. So he waits until a time when everyone else will be out for a while, then he tears down this section of the wall, slips in the box containing all this stuff, and walls it back up again."

"Wouldn't anyone notice? I mean, he couldn't have painted the wet plaster right away, could he?"

"I doubt that Sel or his mother came up here much. After all, this was the head of the family's room."

"Hmm. That would give us an answer to the question we were asking ourselves earlier," Marcie said.

"What question is that?"

"Why Sel only recently began talking about having new evidence regarding the murders. What if he didn't know about this box of his grandfather's stuff being back there until recently, when the roof began to leak? He pulls down the wall, finds the box, and starts looking through it. That's how he gets the evidence as to the identity of the killer."

"And what if that metal box we found in the desk was originally filled with this stuff?" Kevin said with growing excitement. "And it contained the evidence about who committed the murders? Maybe Sel took it downstairs and stored it in the desk."

"Then what happened?" Marcie asked.

Kevin deflated like a punctured balloon. "Who knows?

Even if all this conjecture is correct, the most we've figured out is where the evidence might have been in the past. That doesn't help us to know where it is now. The murderer might have it, or Sel could have taken it out of the box and hidden it somewhere else."

Marcie reached over and patted his shoulder. "Don't get discouraged. I think we're starting to figure things out bit by bit. Look, I'm going to take some pictures. After all, that's what we're supposed to be doing here. Why don't you check quickly through this stuff again just in case there's something else here that gives us a clue, then put the box back where you found it."

Marcie went out to the SUV and got her camera. Back in the house she took pictures of every downstairs room, making sure to get several of the living room with the desk in the shot. She doubted that any of these would ever be used in a story if one did get written, but since it was a digital camera, she would download the pictures onto her laptop tonight. Maybe staring at the pictures on the screen would give her some new ideas, she thought. But somehow she doubted it.

She headed out to the barn, flashlight and camera in hand, knowing that a photo of the hanging beam would be essential for the story. She took a few shots of the outside of the barn from different angles. The one showing the ramshackle farmhouse lurking in the background seemed to be the most ominous and dramatic. Regretting that she hadn't brought along a pair of work gloves to protect her hands, Marcie went around to the front of the barn. She managed to get a grip on the door she had seen Sel pull open. Using all of her weight she managed to drag it back along the ground until there was a large enough space for her to slip inside.

Marcie turned on the flashlight, relieved that she would be able to see the obstacles in front of her this time. The smells were still as stifling as she remembered, but what she noticed even more this time was the silence inside the barn. Although it had hardly been noisy in the empty farmyard, once inside the barn, the absence of sound was like a feeling of pressure on the sides of her head, an active force trying to cut her off from the outside world. *Odd, because I can see daylight through the boards,* Marcie though. *It must be all the hay that deadens the sound.*

Keeping the flashlight pointing toward the floor so she could dodge the scattered hay bales and pieces of equipment, Marcie made her way toward the back of the barn. When she estimated that she had gone far enough, she flashed the light up at the roof. After hunting around for a few seconds, she found the end of the beam. Carefully putting the flashlight down on the floor right in front of her where she could easily find it again, Marcie slipped the camera strap off her shoulder. Half guessing where she should shoot in the shadowy barn, Marcie held the camera away from her, aimed it in the direction of the beam and pushed the button. A burst of light cut through the darkness.

Marcie studied the shot in the viewing frame on the back of the camera. It looked as if she had been pretty lucky the first time. Both ends of the beam were in the frame. But there was something odd. Marcie put the camera back over her shoulder and picked the flashlight off the floor. She ran the light along the beam until she found the spot, then slowly brought the light down in a straight line. Something was hanging from the center of the beam. Marcie walked forward, keeping the light directly in front of her. She lost track of where she was for a moment and gave a grunt of surprise as the top of her head brushed against something. A cobweb? she wondered, backing away in disgust She reached up to brush it out of her hair, and her hand came into contact with a circle of rope. It was a noose.

She gave a small grunt and jumped back, then staggered several feet, stumbling and almost falling. When Marcie finally forced herself to use the flashlight again, she saw what looked to her like an authentic hangman's noose dangling from the beam.

That couldn't be the rope used to hang Sel, could it? she wondered. Surely the police would have taken that away as evidence. But if it wasn't the noose that had been used on Sel, then someone must have returned to the barn to set up this one. The silence of the barn was broken by a gentle, rustling sound from behind a stack of bales in the corner.

Marcie stayed frozen in place, hoping that if she remained still long enough, whatever was there would ignore her. She stared into the shadows until her eyeballs became dry, and slowly she began to imagine that three dark shapes had separated themselves from the general darkness in the corner of the barn.

Marcie glanced up at the beam and for a dizzying moment thought she could see a dark figure hanging from the noose. *None of this can be real,* she told herself. She spun around and began running toward the door. But a dark figure was blocking her way. She charged into it, convinced that it was only another horrible figment of her imagination. But strong arms closed tightly around her.

Chapter Ten

"Marcie, Marcie, it's me, Steve McDermott."

Marcie heard a distant voice repeat that sentence several times before it registered. She had begun struggling as soon as the arms enclosed her, hitting out wildly at whoever or whatever was holding her. But the more she fought, the more tightly she was held.

"Calm down, Marcie. You'll hurt yourself."

Exhaustion finally took over, and she stopped fighting long enough for McDermott to half guide and half carry her out of the barn and into the sunlight. She stood very still for a long moment, stunned by what had happened to her and relieved to find that it really was McDermott and not some horrible apparition. Steve McDermott waited with a concerned expression, watching her carefully until he was sure that she was able to answer questions.

"What was going on in there, Marcie?" he asked.

115

Marcie took a deep breath that threatened to become a sob. She turned it into a cough so as to appear more in control. She regained her composure and explained about the noose, spending more time on it than it actually deserved because that was at least real. Marcie then went on to briefly mention the shadows she had seen. When she was done, she shook her head.

"I'm sure it was just some kind of hallucination. Probably the shock of seeing the noose and being closed up in the barn brought it on. I have a tendency toward claustrophobia." She gave Steve a weak smile. "Sorry to seem like such a goof."

McDermott laughed. "You seem just fine. I'm sure that running into me lurking back in the shadows like that was just icing on the cake."

"I did think for a moment that you were a ghost," Marcie admitted.

"Sorry to surprise you like that. I had some time off at the office and thought I'd come out here to see how the two of you were getting on. Now I'm glad I did. As Sel's executor I'm responsible for this property until his will is settled. If vandals are coming out here and putting up nooses, maybe I'd better hire someone to look after the place."

Marcie heard the screen door slam and saw Kevin coming across the farmyard. Steve quickly told him what had happened. He even told Marcie's story in such a way as to make it sound possible that someone or something—an animal, perhaps—had actually been the cause of what she saw in the barn. The men decided to open both doors of the barn and conduct a thorough search. After several minutes of hard work they accomplished the task.

The sunlight poured into the barn, pushing the shadows into the farthest recesses and making it seem smaller inside. The pieces of equipment strewn around on the floor and the piled up bales of hay appeared less strange in the daylight. The noose, however, still appeared intimidating as it swung back and forth slowly in the light breeze. A search revealed nothing else unusual. To prove that she had regained control, Marcie took several more pictures. In the end she was glad that they had investigated. Just as putting a light on in a dark bedroom after a nightmare can make it less frightening, seeing the barn in daylight had helped take away some of the terror of her experience.

"I'll call Chief Roylston and let him know about the noose," McDermott said as they walked back toward the farmhouse.

"Someone must have purposely put that noose there. The police wouldn't have left behind the one used on Sel, would they?" Marcie asked.

Kevin chuckled. "The Doric police may not be Scotland Yard, but I doubt even they would be that incompetent."

"Someone came out later and put the noose up," Steve said, frowning. "Probably just a prank. It looks like the sort of thing kids might do."

"Or it could have been put there purposely to scare us off," Marcie said.

Steve frowned. "Other than the three of us, who would have known that you would be here today?"

Marcie opened her mouth to say that Chief Roylston knew they'd be there sometime soon, but she decided not to tell Steve the doubts they had with regard to the chief of police.

She checked her watch and turned to Kevin. "It's one o'clock. I guess we'd better be getting back to the inn."

Kevin said good-bye to Steve and handed him the key to the farmhouse. He began walking toward the SUV. Marcie turned to Steve to say good-bye. He took a step toward her and put a hand on her arm.

"Marcie, I don't want you to worry about what happened in the barn today."

"You mean about going crazy and thinking I was seeing ghosts? Yeah, I'm sure that's nothing to worry about," she said with a quick laugh.

"I've lived up this way long enough to know that some people are more sensitive to this stuff than others. There have probably always been some people who pick up sensations more than others do. Just like some people have better eyesight or hearing, some are able to detect certain kinds of vibrations from things that have happened in the past."

Marcie frowned. "I doubt that it was anything as mysterious as all that. I was just nervous and let my imagination run away with me."

Steve smiled and put his hands on both her arms and looked into her eyes. "You're probably right. I just want you to know that this does happen to people. You aren't the first, and you won't be the last. And this is most likely the only time something like this will ever happen to you. Once you're home, you'll think back on this and find it hard to believe that it ever happened. So don't worry about it."

Marcie smiled, wondering why he was making such a big deal out of the episode. "I appreciate your saying that. Anyway, I'm sure it was nothing more than getting worked up too much and letting things spook me."

When she got into the SUV, Kevin asked, "What was that all about?"

"Steve just wanted to reassure me that I'm not going crazy."

"So it's 'Steve' now, is it?"

Marcie glanced at Kevin to see if he was joking, but his expression said that he was on the verge of getting angry. Marcie decided this wasn't a discussion she wanted to have. The day had been hard enough as it was; she didn't want to deal with Kevin's jealousy.

They drove back to the inn in silence.

"Are you going to get some lunch?" Marcie asked, as they walked in the front door.

Kevin shook his head. "I'll pick up something to eat later. I have a few other errands to run." He started to turn away, then changed his mind. "Why don't we get together for dinner tonight?"

"Sounds fine. Too bad I promised the chief that I'd leave tomorrow. I've still got a day before I have to head north, so now I'll have to find another place to stay outside of Doric."

"I'd invite you to stay with me, but I think you'd get pretty tired of having my father interrogate you about your job, while my mother grilled you about your intentions."

Marcie smiled. "As attractive as you make it sound, I think I'll pass. I'll ask at the desk. Maybe they can recommend a place that's on my route."

After they parted in the hallway outside the dining room, Kevin went up to his room, called Chief Roylston, and told him about finding the noose in the barn. He wasn't going to rely on Steve McDermott to fit it into his schedule, but McDermott had already beaten him to it. Roylston assured him that they had indeed removed the rope used to hang Sel and sent it to the state forensics lab. As Kevin had expected, the chief told him the noose was probably just a prank, and that it sounded like the kind of stunt that teenage boys with too much time on their hands would pull. He was a little short-handed at the moment, he said, but he did promise to send someone out to take a look around the farm in the next day or so.

He asked Kevin if they had spotted anything else unusual at the farm, and Kevin had said no. Not a complete lie, because, as Kevin told himself in self-vindication, the box of grandfather Quentin's memorabilia wasn't unusual except to someone working with the same theory that he and Marcie had. The chief ended up sounding like the sheriff in an old Western by saying that he expected Marcie and Kevin to be out of town by the next morning.

Kevin stretched out on the bed, his feet dangling over the end. He stared at the ceiling for moment and relaxed. He always thought better stretched out on his back. Although he had told Marcie that the noose was most likely a prank and had given her the same line of reasoning Roylston had given him, he had serious problems with that theory. Those barn doors were hard to open. Only the most dedicated prankster would have made the effort. And although he was no expert, that noose had looked like a pretty authentic hangman's noose to him. How many kids would have the knowledge or patience to tie one?

He hadn't expressed his reservations to the chief because he suspected that Roylston wasn't really interested in vigorously pursuing the case. He'd go through the motions for a few more days, then quietly let it die. When they didn't hear any more, folks might even begin to assume that it was a suicide, since Sel was such a strange old guy. And if the lab report did show barbiturates in Sel's system, it might easily be dismissed as an unfortunate case of someone mixing drugs and alcohol in order prepare himself for committing suicide. Unlikely, perhaps, but not impossible to believe. Especially when it would spare the town lots of bad publicity.

Kevin reached behind his head and put his hands around the sides of the headboard. He pulled and stretched until the wood began to creak ominously. When he let go, he smiled to himself. This was just the kind of story that would prove to his father as well as everyone else how good he really was. It would establish his credentials. The people working for the *Courier* would say, "He may be the son of the owner, but he's earned his chops as a real reporter."

But Marcie was right: to break this story wide open, he'd need to find out who had murdered those men over sixty years ago and how that was connected to Sel's death. He checked his watch. In less than an hour Jack Brill, his contact at The Lonesome Pine, would be starting his shift. That gave him time to catch some lunch, then stop by to see if Jack had turned up any more information for him.

After what he had seen at the farm, it was more important to him than ever to make a success of this case. Steve McDermott was obviously interested in Marcie. Only by breaking a big story would he have any chance of competing with him.

After leaving Kevin by the registration desk, Marcie went into the dining room with every intention of having lunch. But as soon as she entered the room, the smell of food made her stomach do a flip-flop, and she realized that she was still too tense from her experience at the farm to have a hot meal. As she looked around the dining room, which was much more crowded than it ever was at night, probably with locals, Marcie also decided that she didn't feel like eating alone, surrounded by strangers.

She asked the hostess if it would be possible for her to have lunch in her room and told her that all she wanted was a sandwich. The young woman said that although they didn't technically have room service, the kitchen might be able package up something for her to take to her room. She went off to check with the cook. She returned a few minutes later to ask if a turkey sandwich and a green salad would be adequate, and Marcie gratefully told her that it would. The hostess suggested that Marcie wait in the lobby, and she would bring the food out to her when it was ready.

As Marcie left the dining room to go across the hall to the lobby, she heard an urgent hissing sound. She glanced to her left and saw Mrs. Evans, the older woman who had given her directions to the Hayes farm, standing behind the registration desk, waving for her to come over.

As she approached the desk, Mrs. Evans, who had short gray hair and bright blue eyes, motioned for Marcie to come closer and then whispered in a low voice, "Sorry I had to rat you out to the police yesterday. My daughter heard me giving you directions to Sel's farm, so I couldn't keep mum."

"That's okay," Marcie said, smiling to herself at the woman's conspiratorial manner.

"By the way, my full name is Mabel Evans." A thin hand extended across the desk, and Marcie gave it a gentle shake. "How are you enjoying your stay?"

"It's a very nice inn," Marcie said politely.

"If it were up to me, it would be decorated differently, but I can't tell my daughter what to do. I'm not much more than a guest here myself." The woman leaned even closer until Marcie could smell the scent of her face powder. "I hear you're interested in the hanging men."

Marcie admitted that was true.

"You know, I was only a child, but I remember the big fuss when those men were murdered. Our parents tried to keep it to themselves because they didn't want us to have nightmares, but you know how children are. That was all we talked about at school for months. I think some of the boys even played at hanging each other. It was just lucky that none of them ended up dead."

Marcie nodded. "I'm sure it was a big shock to the town."

"But kind of exciting too." The woman's eyes twinkled. "Someone said that you might be writing a story about it for a magazine."

"Roaming New England."

"Oh, I read that. I love those recipe ideas for locally grown foods."

Marcie made a mental note to tell Amanda that the new magazine on New England cuisine might be a hit after all.

"I don't know if I really have enough material for a story," Marcie said. "So far I don't know much more than what was in the newspaper sixty years ago."

She wasn't going to tell the woman about her meeting with Rachel Heller. Marcie could easily imagine anything she said being quickly spread throughout the town on a senior citizen's grapevine.

"Maybe I can help you," Mabel said with a sly smile.

"Do you know something about what happened?" Marcie asked.

"I don't personally, but there's a woman named Ellen Barkum who could probably tell you plenty. She was a real good friend of Felicia Hayes, Sel's mother. In fact, she and Felicia were sort of competitors at one time for Rudy's attention. He was a real good-looking boy."

"Rudy?"

"Rudolf Hayes, but everyone called him Rudy. That was Sel's father."

"Even though they both wanted to marry Rudy, and Felicia got the prize, so to speak, they stayed friends?" asked Marcie.

"Yes. Of course, it probably didn't hurt that Rudy turned out not to be such a big prize," Mabel said with a small smile. "Wasn't really his fault, I suppose. He was one of those good-looking but weak sorts. Always needed someone to tell him what to do. Quentin pretty much ran the farm even after he officially turned it over to Rudy. Then Rudy got drafted, and Quentin was back in charge. Don't get the wrong idea: it's not that he didn't love the boy; he doted on him—too much, maybe. That's why Rudy never grew a backbone."

"How did Felicia get along with Quentin?" asked Marcie.

"You'll have to ask Ellen. I was too young to hear about adult stuff like that."

"Where can I find Ellen?"

"She's close to ninety now, but she still lives by herself," Mabel said regretfully, as if living on her own was something she wished for daily. "Let me get my book, and I'll write down her address for you."

A large black handbag materialized from under the counter, and after looking through a couple of pockets with an increasingly distressed expression, Mabel pulled a pink address book out of the purse and smiled with relief.

"It's always in the last place you look," she said. "My

daughter tells me that I shouldn't keep my pocketbook under the counter because anyone could steal something out of it when I have to go to the bathroom. But I never have more than a few dollars in it, and I need to have my things with me."

Marcie nodded and smiled. Since she rarely carried more than a wallet and her cell phone, Marcie wasn't exactly sure what *things* Mabel meant. But she wouldn't have been surprised if the woman kept a .38 in there right next to her tissues.

The woman thumbed through several pages, stopping a few times along the way to say something to herself. She must have become aware that she was doing it because she looked up at Marcie and said, "Sorry, my dear, but I'm afraid that I get lost in my own thoughts when I go through this book. Each name brings back memories. Many of these people have been gone for heaven knows how long, but I can't bear to cross out their names. Somehow that would make it seem final."

A few seconds later, the woman slid the book across the counter and pointed to Ellen Barkum's name.

"She's still at the same address, and I imagine she has the same phone number."

Marcie copied down the information and thanked Mrs. Evans.

"I hope it helps," the woman replied. Then her focus sharpened. "And in return, I'd like to know as much as you feel comfortable telling me about what you discover. The hanging men have been sort of . . . well . . . hanging over this town for years. Whenever those of us who go back that far get together for very long, eventually we start to talk about it. But, of course, we're just saying the same old things over and over again. I'd really like to be able to tell my friends something new."

Marcie looked into the twinkling eyes and could see how much it meant to her.

"I'll be sure to send you a copy of anything I write about the hanging men," Marcie promised.

Chapter Eleven

Kevin drove through the center of Doric. About a quarter of a mile out, he turned off the main road into a gravel driveway that led into the parking lot in front a long, log-cabin style building. As he pulled in, Kevin recalled what he had heard about the place. In the 1920s a fellow from down in New York City had decided that he wanted to spend his retirement with the clean air and simple people of rural Vermont. Having some extra money and a vision that the automobile would change the country, he decided to build one of the first motels in the region and called it Pine Grove Cabins. The building that was now a bar had served as the office and restaurant, and in the pine grove behind, he had two rows of cabins constructed, each with one room and a bath.

Like many visionaries, he had the right idea but was a couple of decades ahead of his time. Bankrupt in a few years, he lost the property to a local gangster during

128

Prohibition. The main building became a restaurant and speakeasy, while the cabins were rumored to be tiny houses of ill repute. The end of Prohibition and a wave of civic-mindedness during the Depression led to the closing of the establishment. But a few years later a local businessman reopened the main building as a restaurant and bar. Over time the cabins, which went unused, were stripped of their useful materials, and what was left gradually deteriorated, until now all that remained were two rows of shallow holes overgrown with vegetation, giving it the look of a Neolithic burial site. Although it had gone through several changes of ownership over the last seventy years, the main building continued in use as a favorite local watering hole.

Hanging from a wooden pole by the front door was an elaborate carving of a pine tree that the locals said had been done by an itinerant craftsman who had worked in the area on a WPA project in the late 1930s. Whether the sign preceded the name or the other way around was a matter of dispute among local old-timers, but it was certain that the place had been known as The Lonesome Pine since then.

There were two doors into the building. One took you into the bar, the other into the restaurant. An interior wall divided them from each other. About two-thirds of the building was devoted to the bar, but as Jack Brill had told Kevin, the sale of food hardly justified giving the restaurant even a third of the space. Very few people came there primarily to eat, and the restaurant usually ended up holding the overflow from the bar on a busy night.

The door to the bar was open, since it was a warm

afternoon, and as Kevin approached, the pungent aroma of stale beer and cleaning products greeted him. When he entered, he was momentarily blinded by the darkness. Heavy curtains on the front windows and walls of authentic dark knotty pine gave the place a shadowy, hunting-lodge quality that the moose head mounted over the bar did nothing to dispel.

Since it was almost three in the afternoon, whatever lunch crowd the place got had already left. Two men sat at the far end of the bar with beers in front of them, watching the rerun of the Red Sox game of the day before. They glanced over in curiosity when Kevin came in but soon returned their eyes to the television.

"What'll it be?" Jack Brill asked, turning from the sink where he was washing glasses. He was a thin guy in his thirties with bushy black hair.

"Club soda with a twist of lime."

Jack nodded. He dried his hands and went down to the other end of the bar. In a couple of minutes he returned with Kevin's drink.

"That'll be three-fifty."

Kevin handed him a ten. "Keep the change. Let me run some questions by you."

Jack looked down at the guys at the end of the bar to check that they were focused on the game. He lowered his voice. "I'm not sure I should be talking to you. Chief Roylston was in here yesterday, and he was pretty ticked that I was passing along information to the *Courier*."

"There's nothing illegal in talking to a reporter."

"Yeah. But if Roylston tells my boss that's what I'm

doing, I could be out of a job. A bartender is like a priest, you know—people expect what they say to remain confidential."

"I'm only going to ask questions about people who are dead. I don't think they care about confidentiality."

"Well, I guess you can ask," Jack said, relenting.

Kevin paused to organize the questions in his mind. "When did Sel first start talking about the hanged men?"

"That goes back before my time. Some of the regulars would moan whenever he got off on the topic, because they said he'd been talking about it from when he was a kid."

"But he didn't always say that he had new information?"

Jack wiped his hands on a towel. "I'm not exactly sure when he began with that. I'd guess not more than six weeks ago. A little while after that I heard him telling some of the guys that he'd written to this magazine about the hanging men, and how it was interested in publishing the story. That's when I called you. Then, a couple of weeks later, he said that a reporter was coming up to take a look at the barn."

"Did he give any hint what this new information was?"

"He said that he knew who had done the killings and why."

"His old drinking buddies must have been pretty interested to hear that," Kevin said.

Jack smiled and shook his head. "I don't think anyone really believed him. Sel wasn't the most level-headed guy, even when he was sober. You never could tell when he was telling you the truth or something that he'd made up. But he talked about it so much that after a while some of the old men who'd been around here when it happened started to ask him questions, half kidding, you now, but still curious about whether he really had something."

"What did Sel tell them?"

"Nothing. The more they pressed him for details, the quieter and more agitated he got. You could see that it was hurting him inside not to say anything, but he wouldn't. That's when I started to half believe him. I figured that if he was lying, then he would just make up more lies to keep their interest."

"Did the other guys believe him?"

Jack shrugged. "Most of them lost interest when he wouldn't tell them more, but I think one guy who knew Sel better than most figured he might be on to something."

"Can you give me his name?"

Jack frowned.

"I'm not asking you to give me any personal information about the guy. If I go to see him, I'll just say that I heard he was a friend of Sel's, and I wanted his reaction to his buddy's death."

"Ben Shuster. He lives in the senior-citizen housing on the north end of town."

Kevin finished his club soda and began to slide off the bar stool. Then he remembered that he had promised Marcie to ask about Sel's mother. "Did Sel ever mention anything about his mother?"

"Sure. Sometimes when he was down, he'd talk about how his father got killed in the war and then his mother disappeared."

"Disappeared?"

Jack shrugged. "Sounded more to me like she got fed up with living out at that farm with Sel and his grandfather and took off. Maybe Ben would know more about it."

Kevin nodded and started to leave.

Jack motioned for him to come back toward the bar. He dropped his voice even lower. "You know, I think you're wrong about this whole thing."

"What do you mean?" Kevin asked.

"You don't think Sel committed suicide. Am I right?"

"I'm not convinced that he did."

"You think someone killed him because of what he knew?"

Kevin shrugged.

"Well, there might be another reason for someone to want him dead. And it has nothing to do with the hanging men."

Kevin slid back onto the stool.

Jack checked out the two men at the end of the bar to make sure they were concentrating on the game.

"This *is* sort of confidential stuff."

"I'll see that the *Courier* gives you a nice bonus this month," Kevin promised.

"Yeah. Well, it's not like people don't know about it already if they keep their ears open," Jack said, as if rehearsing what he would say if he ever got called onto the carpet for passing along information. "You know that place where Sel worked?"

"Doric Farm and Garden."

Jack nodded. "Well, Sel had a problem there a while back."

"What kind of a problem?"

"The way I heard it, some stuff took a walk out of the warehouse where Sel worked a couple of evenings a week. Sel was by himself, only one other guy was on duty, and he was up front in the store and wouldn't know what was happening around back."

"So what was going on?" Kevin asked.

Jack leaned across the counter. "All I know is that Bill Turner was involved."

"Should I know who he is?"

"He's the closest thing Doric has to a professional crook. I don't know the details, but from what I've heard, the chief caught Turner with five brand-new John Deere riding mowers in the back of his pickup leaving the Farm and Garden after hours one night. It seemed like quite a coincidence that the chief happened to be outside waiting. The rumor was that Sel set Turner up."

"Why would he do that?"

Jack shrugged. "You could try asking Bob Lambert. He's the owner of the place.

Kevin stood. "If you hear anything more, let me know."

"And there will be a bonus for me this month?"

"Guaranteed."

Jack glanced down the bar at the two guys still engrossed in their game, "Remember. If anyone asks, you didn't hear any of this from me."

Kevin smiled. "I've already forgotten where it came from."

"So what are we going to do tomorrow?" Kevin asked, cutting into his prime rib and holding a piece up to see if it was done the way he liked it.

Marcie was looking out the window at the May evening, enjoying the shadows that the setting sun cast across the lawn behind the inn. She had been purposely trying to focus on something other than the hanging men since her experience of that morning, and she felt a moment of irritation at Kevin's cheerful willingness to return to the topic.

"I made a reservation for tomorrow night at a motel right outside of Montpelier. I figured that I'd work in my room until checkout time, then drive up and browse the city," Marcie said.

"No time," Kevin said.

"What?"

"We've got people to interview tomorrow. It's going to be a busy day."

"We promised the chief that we'd give up on all this if he let us take pictures of the Hayes farm. We can't go back on that."

Kevin cut open his baked potato and put a dollop of sour cream in the middle. "That's not what we promised him. We promised to leave town, not give up the investigation."

"But the implication—"

"An implication isn't a promise. Now that you've heard about this Ellen Barkum person, you have to follow up.

Don't you want to find out what happened to Felicia Hayes?"

"I was going to give Barkum a call."

Kevin shook his head emphatically. "That's not a substitute. You have to look someone in the eye to do a good interview. How can you gauge whether a person is telling the truth when you can't see her expression? Besides, older people like visitors. She'll open up to you more because you took the trouble to show up."

"Okay. Let's say I do come back to Doric to see her. What are you going to be doing?"

"I'm heading out to Doric Farm and Garden."

"The place where Sel worked."

Kevin nodded. "I'm hoping that Robert Lambert, the owner, will tell me about whatever was going on between Sel and Bill Turner."

"Turner, the professional crook," Marcie said, repeating what Kevin had reported from his meeting with Jack Brill. "I hope it doesn't turn out that Sel was killed because he was involved in a plot to steal lawn mowers. That would be a real disappointment."

"I know. I kind of doubt it, though. Even if Bill Turner is bad enough that he would kill Sel for some business scheme that went bad, I can't imagine that the guy would go to the trouble to hang him."

"He might have if he wanted it to look like suicide. Turner is a local crook, so he probably knows the story of the hanging men."

Kevin paused with a piece of meat halfway to his mouth and shrugged. "I guess we'll just have to follow the evidence wherever it leads. One way or the other, we'll find out the truth."

"I suppose," Marcie said. "But it's not going to be much of a story for me if we can't connect Sel's death to the hanging men."

Kevin pushed his hair off his forehead and grinned. "Let's not give up on that angle yet. Why don't you see if you can talk to Ben Shuster tomorrow as well? I checked, and he's in the phone book. I'm not sure how long it will take me to run down this Turner lead."

"Shuster is Sel's old friend from the bar?"

"Right. According to Jack, if Sel confided in anybody, it would be in this Shuster guy."

"What should I tell him about how I got his name? You don't want me to mention that I got his name from Brill, do you?"

Kevin shook his head. "Tell him that you're writing an article about the history of the Hayes farm, and you heard from some people that he was a friend of Sel's, so you'd like to interview him for the story. Most people want to see their names in print."

"Okay. When do you want to get together tomorrow to compare notes?"

"How about for lunch?"

"Where?"

"Right here."

Marcie groaned.

"Don't worry about Roylston," Kevin said. "He can't reasonably expect you to leave town before check-in time at your motel. That won't be before three o'clock."

"When are you leaving Doric?"

"Tonight, actually," he said, grinning sheepishly at being caught out. "I've already checked out of the inn, and my bag is in the car. I can't afford another night."

"Oh, great. You run off and leave me to explain to the chief of police why I'm still hanging around."

Kevin grinned. "Don't worry. I'll be back in Doric tomorrow to see Bob Lambert. My neck will be on the line right along with yours."

"But tonight you're back with the folks," Marcie said.

She hadn't meant it to sound critical, but Kevin blushed.

"Yeah. I know it's not ideal. If this story works out, maybe I won't be doing it much longer."

"Why's that?"

"Once I've proven that I can break a big story on my own, then I'll have earned the right to work on the newspaper. Nobody will be able to say that I got the job just because of my father."

"And that's really important to you?"

"Of course."

"Because you'll have proven something to your father?"

Kevin thought for a moment. "I guess that's part of it. I want my father to have respect for me. Wouldn't you want to earn your father's respect?"

Marcie shrugged. "I'd never even try."

After saying good-bye to Kevin in the lobby with what amounted to a friendly hug and a promise to get together the next day, Marcie went upstairs to her room.

She pushed open the door and turned on the light. Her foot slipped slightly on the wood floor as she stepped inside. She looked down and saw a white envelope under her foot with her last name typed on it. She picked it up and opened the sealed flap.

There was a single sheet of paper inside. She opened it up. Typed in all capital letters it read: GET OUT OF TOWN OR END UP HANGING LIKE THE OTHERS.

At first she almost laughed. For an instant the whole thing seemed to be a sick joke. It was almost a parody of a threatening letter. The kind of thing you'd groan at in a B movie. But then the knowledge sank in that someone had actually come up to her room and stood right on the other side of the door with the intention of threatening her life. With shaking hands, Marcie quickly made sure the door was locked and the safety chain in place; then she sat down on the bed.

What am I going to do about this? she wondered. *If Kevin were still here, I'd rush right up to his room and show it to him.* Suddenly she felt an almost physical ache at the thought of how alone she was. Should she call Chief Roylston? But he knew her room number. Maybe he was the one who had slipped the note under her door, just to make sure that she actually did leave town instead of staying around urging him to solve Sel's murder.

Marcie took a couple of deep breaths. She stood, stretched into a gentle back bend, then jumped up and down several times. She'd discovered, going back to her years on the college field-hockey team, that a little warming up helped to offset a case of nerves. She felt her breathing increase, and slowly her mind began to calm. The first order of business was to try to find out how this note got delivered.

It took some effort to take the chain off the door and unlock it. When Marcie pulled it open, she half expected to see her worst nightmare standing in the hall, waiting to pounce on her. But the hallway was empty. She carefully locked the door behind her and went down to the desk. She was pleased to see that her friend, Mabel Evans, was on duty.

"I found this note under my door," Marcie said, carefully keeping the note out of arm's reach. She didn't want anyone else to read it, or surely the contents would be all around Doric by the next day. "I was wondering how it might have gotten to my room."

"Oh, I put it there, my dear."

"You?" Marcie said.

"Well, not me precisely. I don't like to climb the stairs unless I have to these days. I sent one of the girls up with it."

"Where did you get it?"

"I found it right here on the desk with your name on it. It must have been placed there when you were having dinner. So I just sent someone up with it so you'd be sure to get it as soon as you returned to your room."

"You didn't see who delivered it."

"No. I was downstairs in our banquet room getting things ready. Tonight is the monthly Chamber of Commerce dinner meeting."

"Would anyone else have noticed who dropped it off?"

"I very much doubt it. The lobby and the hallway were

filled with people attending the meeting." She smiled. "I'm afraid that my daughter isn't accustomed to handling large crowds. Every month it's the same thing. We run late getting the banquet room all ready for them, so they have to wait up here for ten or fifteen minutes. There were probably thirty or more people milling around, and all the girls who weren't in the dining room were downstairs setting up."

Marcie frowned.

"Is there anything wrong?" Mabel asked anxiously.

"No, not really," Marcie said with a faint smile. "The person who wrote the note must have thought I'd know his or her handwriting, because it isn't signed."

"How annoying," the woman said. "I get the same thing on the phone, where people call and just start talking as if I should recognize the voice. That's very impolite."

"Yes. Well, thanks for your help."

"I don't mean to pry, but are you going to see Ellen Barkum tomorrow?" Mabel asked.

Marcie paused. Getting out of town had suddenly taken on a new importance. Before, it had been just a matter of satisfying Chief Roylston by checking out of the inn but remaining in town to do her interviews. The person who had composed the note, however, had meant, *Get out, and stay out.* Was she going to leave town in the morning and give Kevin a call telling him that he was on his own? After all, he had a better chance of getting a good story out of this than she did. Why should she take any chances? Then the image came into her mind of her father giving her a contemptuous look whenever she admitted to being afraid of something.

"Yes," Marcie said to Mrs. Andrews. "I'm going to see Ellen Barkum tomorrow."

"Good. Tell her I said hello."

Marcie nodded and began to walk away. Then she stopped.

"Is Chief Roylston attending the Chamber of Commerce meeting?" she asked.

"I didn't look for him," Mabel said. "But all the public officials come to the meetings, so I'd be surprised if he wasn't there. Did you need to see him?"

Marcie shook her head. "I wanted to let him know that I was leaving. But I'll just give him a call tomorrow."

The woman gave her a wink. "It's always best to keep the police informed of your whereabouts."

Marcie smiled but thought that knowing the whereabouts of the police was even more important. As she turned away from the desk, she saw Steve McDermott come rushing in the front door of the inn. He was about to turn to go downstairs to the Chamber meeting when he spotted Marcie and walked across the lobby to greet her.

"We have to stop meeting so unexpectedly," he said, grinning. "How are you doing?"

"Fine," Marcie replied, mustering a faint smile.

"You don't look 'fine' to me," Steve said.

Marcie didn't think that it would wise to tell a public official that she suspected the chief of police to be harassing her into leaving town. Without any solid evidence, that would get her nothing but trouble.

"I'm just a little frustrated at the slow pace of the investigation into Sel's death."

Steve smiled. "Chief Royalston may not be speedy, but he's usually thorough. I'm sure he'll look into all the possibilities on his own timetable."

"I'm sure he means well," Marcie said, "but I was just wondering whether he has the kind of experience necessary to solve this type of case."

"We don't get many killings around here, but the chief has been in law enforcement for over twenty years. He's seen his share of bad things. Plus, he comes from a family of law enforcement officers. His father was on the force for years. In fact, his grandfather took over the chief's job from my great-grandfather when he retired."

"So his grandfather worked on the murders at the Hayes farm?"

"I'm sure that the entire police force, such as it was in those days, must have been involved. Although I do seem to remember hearing that his grandfather was actually in charge of the investigation."

So, Chief Roylston probably has a personal reason to not want this whole thing reopened, Marcie thought, *because it might make his grandfather look bad.*

McDermott glanced at his watch. "I'm sorry, but I have to go. I'm already late for the Chamber dinner. I've probably already missed the first part of the mayor's speech, although I'm sure he's not done yet," he said, and he rolled his eyes.

"Well, it was nice to see you again. And thanks for being so understanding this afternoon," Marcie said, putting out her hand.

Steve took it in his own. "My pleasure. And perhaps instead of all these impromptu meetings, we could actually plan to see each other. Would you be available for lunch tomorrow? We could get together right her at the inn if that would be more convenient for you."

"Technically I'm not supposed to be in town tomorrow. We promised Chief Roylston that if he let us see the farm, we'd be on our way."

"I don't have much power," McDermott said with a smile, "but I might be able to convince the chief to let you stay a little longer, especially if you're in my custody."

Although she was sorely tempted, Marcie decided that having lunch with Kevin to go over the case should probably take priority. "I've got quite a bit of work to do before I go on to my next town, so I'd better not," she said with genuine regret.

"Why don't I give you my phone number? Give me a call next time you're in Doric, and we'll get together."

Marcie agreed, and they exchanged business cards.

"Well, now I really do have to go downstairs," McDermott said with a sigh. He reached over and gave Marcie's shoulder a squeeze. "Do give me a call when you're in town." Then with a parting wave, he loped off down the stairs.

Marcie went back up the stairs to her room feeling considerably happier than when she had come down. She still had her concerns about whether Chief Roylston was the author of the threatening note, but she now felt that she had a powerful friend in town whom she could turn to if things got worse.

Chapter Twelve

Kevin pulled up to the front door of Doric Farm and Garden just as the doors were being unlocked at 8:30. He'd left his parents' house before dawn and spent time at a small coffee shop along the way, having a large breakfast and looking over his notes. He'd left early to avoid having to explain to his father what he was doing these days. His father pretended not to be paying attention to his comings and goings, but Kevin knew that not much slipped past him. His father had to be generally aware of what he was working on because he had written the story about Sel's death and had been staying in Doric for the last few days. Since Kevin was only a freelancer, his father would be reluctant to officially call him into the office and question him. However, a friendly conversation over breakfast could result in almost the same thing, and he wasn't going to tip his hand until the story was completed.

A short, heavyset man was standing behind the counter as Kevin walked into the store. He was wearing a blue knit shirt that tightly spanned his beach ball of a belly. The shirt had a badge with *Bob* on it.

"Hi," Kevin said. "Are you Bob Lambert?"

"Sure am."

"Then maybe you can help me."

The man smiled. "I'll give it a try. What do you need?"

"I'm a reporter for the *Courier,* and I'm checking out some background information on Seldon Hayes. I understand that he was an employee here."

The man nodded, a wary expression replacing the smile.

"What kind of an employee was he?"

"He was okay for a guy pushing seventy. I can't tell you much more about him than that."

"You were the one who found his body."

The man nodded again, his face grim. "He didn't show up for work, so I stopped by his farm to see what was wrong. I found him."

"Not many bosses would check up on a part-time employee when he didn't show up for work. That was pretty decent of you," Kevin said.

"Sel had his problems, so when he didn't show, I figured that it might be serious."

"What kind of problems?"

"Binge drinking," Bob said. "He'd go along fine for a while, just having a few beers down at The Lonesome Pine. Then all of a sudden he'd start drinking really heavily for weeks in a row and not be able to leave the farm. He ended up in the hospital a couple of times.

When he didn't show up for work, I figured I'd better see how he was doing."

"That's still a lot for a boss to do."

Lambert sighed. "Let's just say that I have some idea of the problem myself. That's why I hired him in the first place."

"Is that why you kept him on even after he got involved with Bill Turner?"

"Where did you hear that?" Lambert said, his voice suddenly hard.

Kevin forced himself not to blush or fuss with his hair as he usually did when nervous. "It's not a secret that Sel was involved in a sting that involved Bill Turner."

"I'm not going to talk any more about this. I want you to leave the store."

"Sure, I can do that," Kevin said amiably. "But when I write my article, I'll have to say that the owner, Robert Lambert, refused to comment on allegations that Sel Hayes' death was related to his involvement with thefts from Doric Farm and Garden."

"Nobody ever alleged that."

"But it kind of makes sense, doesn't it?" Kevin knew that he'd never carry out his threat, but he figured it was a good bluff.

Lambert stared at the countertop as if unsure what to do.

"Look," Kevin said, "I don't want to write an article that will get you bad publicity. Probably whatever Sel was into here had nothing to do with his death. I just want to be able to satisfy myself that I haven't overlooked something."

"If it has nothing to do with his death, you won't write about it?"

"That's a promise."

"My warehouse manager had noticed that a few things had gone missing over the past few months. The inventory sheets weren't balancing out exactly right. We'd be ten bags of feed short at the end of the month or down a half pallet of fertilizer. Things get shifted around in the warehouse and out on the lot, so you wouldn't always notice right away if something was really missing or had just been moved."

"But eventually you knew that stuff was walking?"

Lambert nodded. "And it had to be happening at night, because there was a crew of two and the manager around during the day."

"Sel was alone here for his shift?"

"He came in at six. One of the day crew stayed on until six-thirty. After that Sel was by himself in the warehouse until nine."

"Sounds like hard work for an old guy," Kevin said.

Lambert smiled. "Sel was a lot stronger than he looked. And after seven-thirty there isn't much business even in the spring and summer. He only worked three nights a week. The rest of the time we close at six."

"What did he do in the winter?"

"He only worked seasonally, from April through October."

"Must have been hard for him to make ends meet."

"He had Social Security and a small pension."

"I thought he was a farmer pretty much all his life."

Lambert shook his head. "After his grandfather died

in the early fifties, he got a factory job up near Montpelier. He lived on the farm, but it was never a going concern. I imagine that the taxes must have cost him more than the place was worth, but I guess he wanted to keep it in the family, although I don't know who he planned to pass it on to."

"So you figured out that the stuff was disappearing on Sel's watch?" Kevin asked, getting back to the point.

"Yeah. Actually, I wasn't the one who figured it out. My warehouse manager was so ticked about the stuff going missing that without telling me he began hiding just outside the fence that surrounds the yard to see what was happening. Finally he saw Turner's pickup truck pull into the yard one night, and Sel helping him load it up with fertilizer. When my manager checked the next day, there was no sales slip to cover it."

"What happened then?"

"I was away on a trip the next day or it would have been handled differently, I can tell you that. But my manager felt it was too urgent to wait, and he called the police."

"How would you have handled it?" Kevin asked.

"Look, my manager wasn't a local guy. He was from somewhere out near Albany, so he figured that when you have a thief, you call the cops. Now sometimes you have to do that, but Sel was special. I would have pointed out to Sel that I was doing him a big favor keeping him around, and he should prove that he appreciated it by not stealing my goods. He'd have passed the word on to Turner. That would have put an end to it, and I'd have just written off what I'd already lost."

"Turner would have left it at that. I thought he was a professional."

"I guess, in the sense that it's what he does for a living, but he's pretty small-time. It's sort of a family tradition. His father and grandfather were in the same line of work. He mostly makes money by fencing stuff that even smaller-time crooks bring to him. I suspect he runs a lot of it across into Canada by the back roads."

"So he'd stop stealing from you if you asked him to?"

"Sure. He's just another local guy. He'll steal from his neighbors if they make it easy for him, but let him know that you're on to him, and he'll back off. We get along. He even buys feed from me."

"What happened when the cops got involved?"

"Roylston got real excited, because here was a chance to get the goods on this local legend."

"Did Roylston come up with the idea of a sting of some kind?"

"Yeah. I couldn't talk him out of it. He had my manager's statement of what he saw, so I had to go along. Sel wanted to avoid being involved, but Roylston was ready to charge him unless he cooperated. The chief came up with this plan where Sel would let Turner know about a shipment of John Deere riding mowers coming in. He was to tell Turner that he would arrange to have them left outside overnight in the yard. Turner could cut the lock on the gate, load up, and leave."

"Running right into the waiting arms of the police," said Kevin.

"That was the plan."

"Did something go wrong? Didn't they catch him?"

"They caught him all right. At eleven o'clock he pulled into the yard with one of his cousins to help him, loaded the mowers, and drove out again. The police were waiting for him."

"So I guess Turner had good reason to be angry with Sel."

Lambert shook his head.

"Why not?"

"When they stopped Turner as he was driving out of the parking lot and asked why he had a truckful of mowers, he showed them a bill of sale with a time stamp from three hours earlier, and Sel backed it up with store paperwork. Turner said he'd come by and paid Sel around seven. But he didn't have his truck at the time, so Sel said that he'd leave the gate unlocked. Turner could pick up his merchandise later and lock up when he left. And sure enough, the lock wasn't cut. The police had to let him go."

"Had Turner really paid for the mowers?"

"No one saw him come in except for Sel."

"You must have been out a lot of money."

The man looked at Kevin expressionlessly.

"Unless, of course, you and Turner came to an agreement where he was going to pay you back or return them."

Lambert shrugged. "Like I said, Turner and I get along."

"Roylston must have been embarrassed."

"Yeah. He had most of the police force here to spring the trap, and he came out of it with egg on his face in front of everyone. I wasn't here, but I heard that

Sel was dancing around making it sound like he was being unjustly accused and that he would sue for police harassment."

"Couldn't Roylston at least charge Sel on the fertilizer theft, the one your manager saw?"

"Funny thing. Sel came up with the paperwork for that too. He said it had been misplaced."

Kevin smiled. "And I bet Turner had a sales slip for the fertilizer."

The man nodded.

"What did your warehouse manager say about all that?"

"I'd had to let him go. Downsizing, you know."

Kevin gave the man a long look. "I wouldn't have thought that Sel could manipulate all that paperwork on his own."

Lambert shrugged again.

"The police won't come running out here the next time you cry thief. But I suppose with Sel gone and Turner happy with you, theft won't be a big problem."

The man gave him a small smile. "Yeah. I guess things are looking up."

Marcie put her suitcase into the trunk of her car. She stood by the driver's door and tried to check around her for suspicious activity without being obvious about it. She was by the side of the inn, so the car wasn't fully exposed to the street, which seemed to be empty of traffic anyway. There were two other cars parked in the lot but no sign of other people. She scanned the windows of the inn and didn't see any faces peering out at her. Behind the inn was a wooded area, but the idea of someone sitting out there with binoculars trained on her car struck Marcie as ludicrous. She wasn't sure whether she wanted to be under observation or not. The thought that she was being watched was definitely creepy, but if the person who sent last night's threatening note knew she had left the inn, she might be safer.

Could the note have been left by Chief Roylston? She had asked herself that question over and over again this morning. In the cold light of day, the warm glow of her conversation with Steve McDermott had worn off, and she realized that her problems were still the same. Roylston had already officially suggested that she leave. Would he really stoop to a threatening note just to reinforce her compliance? Somehow that seemed unlikely, even though he had probably had access to the inn's desk. But he also knew her room number, so wouldn't he have personally slid the note under her door? Of course, he could have wanted to conceal his identity by leaving the note at the desk. With complication on top of complication, her mind spun around and around, and Marcie knew that she wasn't going to make any headway toward figuring things out until she had more information.

She got into the car and started the engine. Aside from being spooked at the possibility of being watched, she was also feeling guilty at not giving Amanda a fuller account of the situation on the phone last night. She had told her about leaving the inn—no point in trying to conceal what her travel voucher would eventually reveal anyway—but she hadn't mentioned Chief Roylston's request that she leave for her own safety.

She had simply said that he had allowed her to leave Doric because she was no longer needed as a witness. She had also neglected to mention anything to Amanda about the threatening note under the door, knowing that her friend and boss would have ordered her to get out of town immediately and return to Wells.

She had told Amanda in some detail about the search she and Kevin had conducted of the Hayes farm and what it had revealed about Quentin Hayes' past. They batted back and forth the likelihood that whatever Sel had found in his grandfather's papers must have revealed the identity of the long-ago murderer. Amanda thought that, although it was all rather interesting, it still left them with no idea of what Sel had actually discovered in his grandfather's papers. She had gently suggested that the story was at a dead end, and it was time for Marcie to move on.

Marcie had given her the impression that she agreed. She didn't mention to Amanda that she had interviews in Doric planned for today and instead had told her only of the original plan to go sightseeing in Montpelier.

Deciding that it was time to stop worrying about what was already done, Marcie backed out of the spot and made a left turn out of the parking lot. Her destination was about five miles away in what the locals apparently called North Doric. She had called Ellen Barkum the evening before and arranged to see her this afternoon at her home. She had also phoned Ben Shuster, the lead Kevin had come up with at the bar, and he had agreed to meet her in a coffee shop across the street from the senior housing in North Doric at ten o'clock. So that was her first destination.

Barbara Sharp, who was on the desk as she left that morning, gave her directions. She said that North Doric was really a part of Doric that had clung to its own designation as a stubborn sign of independence. If Marcie followed the road north out of town from the inn for about five miles, she'd come to an intersection with a white church and a small triangular park. That was the traditional center of North Doric. Recently, however, it had been augmented by a surprisingly modern-looking apartment building. That was senior housing, and across the street was a tiny strip mall with a grocery store, drugstore, small restaurant, pizzeria, and a couple of other shops that she couldn't remember.

Barbara Sharp's directions proved accurate, and in about fifteen minutes Marcie found herself in North Doric. It was easy to spot the senior housing because it was by far the largest building around and perhaps the only one constructed in the second half of the twentieth century aside from the stores across the street. Marcie parked the car and walked into the coffee shop, wondering how she would identify Ben Shuster. He had told her last night not to worry about it because he would easily be able identify her. She wasn't exactly sure how, but she hadn't wanted to argue with him.

She stood by the cash register and surveyed the customers. At ten o'clock she had expected the place to be empty, since it was between breakfast and lunch. But more than half the booths were occupied by senior citizens. A younger person was reading out numbers for a large group of them who were playing bingo. At a round table in a corner five men were talking, ignoring the commotion made by the players behind them. No one other than the number caller looked to be under the age of seventy. One of the men at the table stood up and approached Marcie.

"Hi, are you the girl from the magazine?"

"That's right. Marcie Ducasse." She put out her hand. His was hard and callused, indicating that he'd done plenty of manual labor in his life. He had a full head of white hair, and although his shoulders were stooped, she could see that he had once been a physically impressive man.

"I'm Ben Shuster. Why don't we sit over there?" he said, pointing to a booth is the corner farthest from the bingo players. "It gets kind of noisy in here when they get excited."

"Would you like anything to eat?" he asked once they were settled into the wooden booth. "The eggs here are good, and they serve breakfast all day."

Having eaten a big breakfast at the inn before checking out, she turned down the offer.

"Coffee, then?" he asked hopefully.

Realizing that he was trying desperately to break the ice by being a good host, she agreed. She was surprised when Ben got up himself and brought back two heavy china mugs of coffee.

He smiled at her look of surprise. "The owner trusts us. We're pretty much his only midmorning business."

"Looks like a pretty social place."

"Yeah. Most of us live in the senior apartments across the street. The places are nice enough, but it's good to get out once in a while and see other people."

"Do they have a senior center in town?"

"Yeah, they have one down in Doric that we share with the folks in Corinth. Sometimes I go there because you can get a cheap lunch. They have crafts and games in the afternoon." He grinned. "But I'm not really into that stuff."

"It seems nice here."

"Well, Doric is my home. And I'm not sure I've got the energy to start over somewhere else. Not by myself anyway. My wife died a couple of years ago—cancer."

"I'm sorry. It must be hard to adjust to being alone."

He nodded at the table in the corner. "At least I have my friends."

Marcie smiled, wondering how much of a substitute they were for a wife. "Well, as I mentioned on the phone," she began, taking out her notebook, "I want to talk to you about Sel Hayes. I understand that the two of you were pretty good friends."

"I wouldn't say that, but I knew him for a long time."

"How did you meet?"

"I started out on a farm in Doric too. We went to school together, although we weren't friends. I was a few years older. But my family sold out when I was in my early twenties. I took a training course at the local vocational school and got a job as a toolmaker at the same boiler factory where Sel came to work."

"So you were friends on the job?" Marcie asked.

He shook his head. "We'd nod. After all, we knew each

other from around Doric, but Sel worked in a different department. He did assembly. I guess you could say that he was general labor, whereas I was more of a specialist."

There wasn't much inflection in his tone, but Marcie thought she detected a note of pride.

"After we retired, we'd run into each other at The Lonesome Pine. That's when we started to talk more."

"I guess Sel tended to talk a lot?" Marcie asked.

Ben smiled. "After a few beers, you couldn't shut him up. He told a good story, but after you'd heard it two or ten times, it wasn't so interesting. I usually left early when Sel was there, which was most of the time."

"But the last month or so he began telling a new story, didn't he?"

Ben took a sip of coffee and gave her an appraising look. "I thought you wanted to know about Sel as part of a story about the history of his farm."

"Sure. But what happened there sixty years ago is an important part of that."

"You mean all the hanging stuff."

Marcie nodded.

"Sel didn't know much about that. He was just a kid and out at the creek with his granddad when it happened. I heard that story often enough."

"But what about the new story?"

"You mean when he started talking about knowing who killed those men?" Ben stopped, and his eyes widened. "I bet you're that magazine reporter that he was talking about at the bar. The one who was coming out to write that story about the farm."

"I'm the one."

"Well, then, you know more than I do. Sel kept real quiet about what he'd found out, because he figured it would make him some money."

"I wasn't able to offer him enough, so I didn't learn anything. And now he's dead."

Ben shook his head. "I couldn't believe it when I heard that he hanged himself. I always figured that he'd drink himself to death someday. But to hang himself like those guys he saw in the barn . . ." He paused and shook his head. "It was pretty hard to believe that happened. I think what he saw there as a kid always haunted him. You wouldn't think he'd decide to go the same way."

"Maybe he didn't."

"What are you—"

He stopped and stared across the room. Marcie watched as the pieces fell into place.

"You think someone did that to him? Who'd still be around who'd care about what happened over sixty years ago?" he finally asked.

"I figured maybe you could tell me. Didn't Sel give you a hint?"

"All I remember is that when he first stated talking about it, he told me that if he'd known what had happened before his grandfather died, the old man never would have fallen down the attic stairs."

"Why not?"

"Sel said that he would have pushed the old man down the stairs himself."

Marcie thought for a moment. Would Sel be so upset

to find that his grandfather had been involved in the hangings that he'd want to kill him? Sel hadn't struck her as a guy with such a strong craving for justice.

"Didn't he give you any idea who he thought might have hanged those men back in the forties?"

"Nope. He wouldn't talk about it. He'd just slip you a sly look as if to say that you'd be real surprised to find out. To be honest, it got kind of annoying. After a while I stopped talking to him about it."

"What about his grandfather? Could Quentin Hayes have been involved in the murders?"

"Why would he do something like that?"

Marcie explained what they'd discovered about the three men not being soldiers and having done things that could be seen as damaging to men in the military.

Ben frowned. "Yeah. I guess that makes sense. I was only a kid at the time, so I'm not sure what folks were thinking. But why would Quentin care?"

"Didn't his son, Rudy, die in the war?"

"Not exactly. I mean, he was still in the Army when he died, but the war in Europe was already over. He was killed in an automobile accident. Just like General Patton."

"Are you sure?" Marcie said with a sinking feeling.

"That's one story that Sel did tell often enough. I guess he figured that it made his dad sound like some kind of war hero, although I don't think he was ever anywhere near the real fighting."

"And when Rudy died, that would have been after 1944."

"Sure. Long after those guys were strung up in the barn."

Marcie sank back in the booth. There went Quentin's motive for getting involved in the murders. Desperately trying to think of another question that might open a new door, Marcie recalled that Greg, the managing editor at *Roaming New England,* had told her once that questioning was a creative act. People had all sorts of details in their memories, he said, but couldn't recall them unless they were asked just the right question that jogged the information loose. It was like being an archaeologist: If you see something interesting, you have to ask lots of questions to clear away the dirt around it like they do with their little brushes, until the entire story is exposed. You can't just reach in and pull it out. Marcie looked at Ben and wished she could come up with a series of creative little brushlike questions, but all that came to hand was a basic broom.

"Did Sel ever say anything that struck you as odd?"

Ben grinned. "Lots of times. That was Sel." He stopped and thought for a moment. "But the last time I saw him, he did say something a little peculiar even for him. It was after I told him that he should take what he knew to the police."

"What did he say?"

"He laughed and said that would be the last place he would go."

Chapter Thirteen

Marcie parked her car back in the same slot it had occupied that morning next to the inn. After leaving Ben Shuster, she had driven up to Montpelier and spent a few hours walking through the downtown, touring the gold-domed statehouse and poking around in a small book-shop at the other end of the main street. The trip made her feel less as if she had lied to Amanda. For a small city it had a lot to offer, and she'd have preferred to spend a pleasant afternoon there rather than returning to Doric. But she knew that would be giving in to her fears, and nobody ever became a good journalist by doing that.

As Marcie walked into the inn, she paused to glance over her shoulder and saw a police car go past. She couldn't be certain, but it could have been Chief Royl-ston. Was he following her, and was he going to stop at the inn and create a scene because she and Kevin hadn't left town yet?

Kevin was sitting in the lobby watching the door. He jumped up to greet her. She was surprised at how happy she was to see a friendly face.

"I think I saw the chief just drive past the inn," Marcie said.

"We'll deal with that if and when the time comes," Kevin said. "I've got lots of stuff to tell you."

"I've got a few things to tell you too," she replied.

It took all of Marcie's self-control to wait to tell Kevin about the threatening note until after they had ordered. He listened intently, not even picking up a piece of the warm cornbread from the basket in front of them.

"Hmm. You know what this means?" he asked.

Marcie shook her head.

"It means that we're definitely on the right track with this thing. Somebody is getting pretty nervous."

"Right," Marcie snapped, feeling a surge of anger at his indifference. She had at least expected him to say that she should have called him last night, and he'd have returned to the inn immediately. "It also means that someone is threatening my life. It's all very well for you to act as if this is some kind of puzzle we're trying to solve or a mystery dinner where we're trying to guess who killed the chef. But we're not playing here, Kevin. People have ended up really hanging in that barn."

Marcie stopped. She wanted to take a drink of water, but she knew her hands were shaking too much from a mixture of anger and fear to make that possible. Instead she grabbed the end of the table and just stared at Kevin, who blushed and looked down at his plate.

"I'm sorry," he mumbled. "I know that sounded

pretty bad. And I realize that a note like that can be up-setting. But I don't really think you've got anything to worry about."

"Not worry! You don't take this seriously. Well, I do. I've had my life threatened before. I've had people point guns at me, lock me in closets, and even try to burn me alive. I keep coming back because I'm a writer, and weird things are what I write about. But I will not put up with your telling me I shouldn't worry about death threats."

Marcie's throat hurt from whispering so angrily, and her hands had started to shake from squeezing the table. She consciously forced herself to relax her grip. She knew that a lot of her upset had nothing to do with Kevin but was the stress of the past few days coming to a head. She folded her hands in her lap and remained silent except for ordering. Kevin didn't speak either. Time crept by. Finally their food came, a shepherd's pie for Kevin, salmon with dill sauce for herself. They began to eat, but Kevin's eyes never left his plate.

"Well, say something," she finally demanded, when it seemed that he would sit there forever without speaking.

"I didn't know it was my turn," he replied with a grin.

"Don't be cute."

Kevin's face became solemn, and he nodded. "You're right. I'm afraid that's just the way I approach things when I'm nervous. I try to make a joke out of them. But that doesn't mean I'm not taking it seriously on the inside. I'm not sure what we should do about the note. As you said, we can't go to the police, because it might have been Roylston who wrote it. That's even more likely now that we know he had a grudge against Sel."

"What are you talking about?" Marcie asked.

Kevin went on to explain what he had learned at the farm and garden store about Sel's role in the failed sting.

"Okay. I can see why Sel might not have been the chief's favorite person, but would he really have murdered Sel because the guy embarrassed him?" Marcie said; then she paused. "But Bob Shuster did say that Sel was afraid to go to the police."

She went on to tell Kevin about her conversation with Shuster.

"So Sel maybe couldn't go to the police because he'd helped Turner avoid arrest," Kevin said. "That still doesn't get us any closer to figuring out how those guys got strung up in the barn or who killed Sel."

"And Roylston is way too young to have been involved in sixty-year-old murders," Marcie added.

"Maybe Sel figured the chief was protecting the killer."

"Well, we think he's not working real hard to solve the crime because he doesn't want to embarrass the town. I also found out that he has a personal reason to make this case disappear." Marcie told Kevin about her meeting with McDermott in the lobby and finding out that Roylston's grandfather had worked with McDermott on the investigation of the hanging men.

"You seem to be running into Steve McDermott quite a lot lately," Kevin said. Marcie's expression warned him not to pursue the topic. "But that is good information to know," he ended lamely.

"Sel sat out there on that farm by himself a lot," Marcie said. "It wouldn't have taken much for him to start thinking that there was a huge conspiracy to hide whatever happened in the barn years ago. That's probably why he wanted to sell his story to the press."

Kevin nodded. "And from what you heard from Shuster, Sel was really down on his grandfather. Probably because he figured that Quentin was involved in the hangings. He must have found that out from his grandfather's papers, and it changed his whole attitude toward him."

"But why would Quentin have gotten involved in those murders? I'm not convinced that he was such a fanatic that he was willing to kill men just because they had indirectly hurt veterans. The town in general may have despised those three men for what they'd done, even ostracized them, but it takes more than that to be willing to kill them. If Quentin was involved, I think he must have had another reason."

"And Quentin couldn't have done it all by himself, not with only one arm," Kevin added.

"He had to have a partner, but we still don't have enough information to figure out who that might be."

"Maybe this Ellen Barkum will be able to help," Kevin said. "Do you know how to get to her place?"

"She gave me directions from the inn last night."

Kevin hesitated. "Do you want me to go with you, to sort of cover your back?" he asked, using a spoon to scoop up the last of the gravy from his shepherd's pie.

Marcie smiled. "I appreciate the offer. But you probably have something else you want to do."

Kevin nodded. "I got an idea when I went back to the library and did a little more research this morning."

"Was that cute little librarian, Lisa, there?"

"Nope. One of those older witches that she told us about, although the woman seemed nice enough to me."

"Lisa wouldn't think that anyone who made her work was nice."

"Don't be jealous," Kevin teased.

"I'm not," Marcie replied.

She realized, as soon as she said it, that it was true. Her feelings for Kevin had changed, and they were never going to be of the romantic sort. Although they were about the same age, there was something immature about Kevin that made her see him as a younger brother more than as a boyfriend. Maybe it was the way he used his boyish looks to get what he wanted from Lisa, or possibly his jealousy concerning Steve. For whatever reason, she liked him as a friend but was suddenly certain that it was never going to be anything more than that.

Kevin cleared his throat to get her attention. "I decided to see if there were any other people in town who had been directly involved in the incidents that the hanged men were accused of bringing about. I looked through the obituary of the Campbell boy, the kid who got run over by Jake Heller."

"And?"

"Well, he had a younger sister. She's using her married name, Elaine Page, but I managed to track her down through a couple of cousins. I'm going to see her this afternoon. Unless, of course, you want me to go with you."

Marcie thought for a moment, then shook her head. "I'll be okay. I'll go right from here to Ellen Barkum's, then head directly out of town to my motel."

"Do you have time for dessert?" Kevin asked, glancing at a piece of blueberry pie with vanilla ice cream, as the waitress carried it past them to another table.

"Nope," Marcie said, checking her watch.

"I think I'll stay and have some. Give me a call later on this afternoon. We can get together for dinner somewhere near the place you're staying."

"I'll see how things go. I have a lot of driving to do tomorrow, and I want to make it an early night."

Kevin looked at her for a long moment, then managed a faint smile. "Fair enough," he replied.

Ellen Barkum's house was in a neighborhood of small ranch houses off of the main road out of town. They seemed strikingly out of place amid the Capes Cod, Colonials, and old farmhouses dotting the landscape, giving the impression that some suburban developer had gotten his map coordinates wrong and started building without realizing he was in rural Vermont. The neat white ranch house that matched the address Marcie had been given would have looked far more natural in the suburbs of Boston or New York. Surprising as the style of the house was, the person who answered the door surprised Marcie even more. She had expected a little old lady wearing a dress trimmed with lace, but the woman who opened the door towered over her and was wearing jeans and a denim shirt.

"I'm here to see Ellen Barkum," Marcie said.

"You're looking at her."

"Oh, sorry, I just thought—"

"I know, you thought I was her caregiver." The woman gave a short, barking laugh. "I guess in a way I am. I take care of myself. Come on inside."

Marcie went through the door and found herself in the living room. Back in college one of her close friends had paid part of her way through college by going to estate sales, flea markets, and tag sales, purchasing items that she would resell to antique dealers. On free weekends Marcie had frequently gone with her, especially if her friend was on the hunt for furniture and would require another pair of hands to help her load her old pickup truck. So, as she entered the room, Marcie immediately recognized the vintage 1950s stuff, from the kidney-shaped coffee table and the spare chairs with metal frames to the lamps in bright primary colors. She couldn't help mentioning it to Mrs. Barkum. The woman chuckled.

"When Mr. Barkum and I moved in here, it was right after the war. We didn't have much money, so we started out with bits and pieces we got from our relatives. But a few years later we managed to save up enough to start furnishing the place the way we wanted. I always wanted to be modern, so we went all the way to Boston to buy this stuff. I can tell you, we were pretty proud of ourselves."

"You should be. These are wonderful pieces and in excellent condition," Marcie said, sitting down in the chair that the woman had gestured toward.

"We never had any children, or else this stuff would all be kindling by now from them jumping on it. My friends didn't think much of this house or the furniture when we first moved in. They all had big Colonials or Victorians filled with heavy furniture made to last for the ages. 'A tract home with tacky furniture,' they'd say behind my back, as if they didn't know word would get back to me."

The woman paused and stared across the room as if she could hear the people saying it now. She directed her gaze at Marcie and tapped the side of her nose shrewdly.

"But who's laughing now? Those of them who are still around had to sell their big, fine, two-story homes and pay an arm and a leg to move into some assisted-living place where they don't have to climb stairs. And all of that museum furniture either went to their kids who really didn't want it or got given away to charity, while I sit here in my own house with my own stuff."

"You seem to be doing just fine."

The woman nodded her agreement. "Still drive and get around pretty well, except for a little arthritis in the knees. But the most important thing is keeping your spirits up, and I guess going my own way has always taken care of that for me. Maybe I haven't always been popular, but I've always had a good reason to get up in the morning."

"But you did have some friends, like Felicia Hayes."

The woman gave one of her short laughs. "Felicia and I got along real well because neither one of us got along with anyone else. And that's not easy when you live in a small town. I didn't get along because I had my own opinions, and I wasn't afraid to express them. Felicia had a problem that, unfortunately, I never had."

"What was that?" Marcie asked.

"She was beautiful."

"Why was that a problem?"

"Don't be naïve. You're old enough to know how women think. Once Felicia hit sixteen, every woman in town saw her as a little home wrecker. Can't really blame them, the way the men of all ages would drool when she was around. Even in church I swear that Reverend Willett spent more time looking at her than he did at the Holy Word. I guess even the best men can't help it; it's ingrained in their nature."

"That must have made it very hard for her," Marcie said.

Ellen Barkum startled Marcie by winking. "Sure. But don't think that Felicia didn't take advantage of it sometimes. I'm not saying she ever did anything wrong, but she sure could make her eyes go big and wide when she wanted something from one of her male teachers."

"The two of you were in the same class in school together, right? And weren't you both interested in Rudy Hayes?"

The woman smiled softly. "Oh, my, Rudy. Now there was quite a boy. When you looked into those cornflower blue eyes, you could imagine a future filled with all sorts of possibilities."

"A real hottie," Marcie said with a grin.

"Definitely. The problem was that all you were seeing in those eyes was your own reflection, because the boy was as dumb as a stump. I'm not saying he was retarded. It was more like he just couldn't be bothered to think. He'd go along with whatever folks told him to do and seem pretty satisfied. I always wondered exactly what was going on in Rudy's sweet head when he was alone. Maybe all he did was see pretty pictures of himself."

"But you went after him, and so did Felicia."

"That's just a story that's gotten around over the years. Sure, I made a play for Rudy in my junior year, but it was never anything serious. First of all, I never was pretty enough to compete with the other girls who chased after him. And second, I figured out sooner than most that Rudy would turn out to be the kind of guy you'd have to take care of for his whole life. You'd end up doing all the thinking for both of you."

"Didn't Felicia see that?"

"Of course she did. She was at least as smart as I was. She came to me in the middle of our junior year and asked if it was okay with me if she went out with him. She knew Rudy and I had gone out a couple of time, and she was too good a friend to cut me out, even though that's what the girls who hated both of us said later."

"What did you say to her?"

"I told her what he was like. I said that she'd be bored out of her mind in a couple of hours. You can only look at something beautiful for so long; then you want more."

"How did Felicia reply to that?"

"She didn't. Felicia just smiled as if she had a secret that she wasn't going to tell me. We didn't see each other much after that except in class. She spent most of her free time with Rudy. But at the end of our senior year, right after they got engaged, Felicia came to see me one afternoon at home. I can still remember us sitting on the swing on the front porch of my parents' home, drinking lemonade."

"What did you talk about?" Marcie asked after a moment.

Ellen Barkum paused. "Well, I was sitting there going on about this and that. I was trying to be good and not ask her why on God's green earth she was planning to marry Rudy, when she suddenly turned to me with a big smile and said, 'Why don't you ask me?' So I did."

"And?" Marcie urged. "What was her answer?"

The woman sighed, and Marcie was startled to see her chest heave as if she were holding back tears.

"Are you all right?"

"Give me a minute," Barkum said. She took several deep breaths, and slowly her face grew less red.

"You have to understand that this was still the nineteen-thirties. I'm sure that's ancient history to you. And you'd be right to think that things were a lot different then. I had a good family, and we were pretty well off. My dad ran his own drugstore, and that was back when you could make a living 'round here doing that. So, even though I had two older brothers, my folks sent me to college so I could become a teacher. I was lucky. In those days even families with money didn't always figure that a girl needed an education after high school."

Mrs. Barkum stared hard at Marcie to see if she understood, and she nodded.

"Felicia's family didn't have much. Her father was

sickly, as we used to say back then. It covered everything from being lazy to being a drunk. I'm not sure exactly what it meant in his case. There were two boys older than Felicia and three younger. Her mom told her when she was a junior that they were doing her a favor by letting her complete high school. As soon as she graduated, she had to get a job at the textile mill where her mom and her two older brothers worked to help support the family. What she told me on the porch swing that afternoon was that Rudy was her way out of that."

Marcie frowned. "Was that really the better choice?"

"Her looks wouldn't have lasted long in that mill. She'd have probably married someone who worked there and ended up like her mother in a few years' time. The Hayes farm was a thriving business in those days. The place must have looked like paradise compared to the alternative." Ellen sighed. "And, who knows? Maybe she thought, like a lot of women do when they marry, that she could make her man into something. I never saw things that way. When I married my George, I knew what he was, and I was satisfied. Good thing too, because he was pretty much the same when he died as the day I married him. Changing a man is like trying to straighten a bent board: You get very little result for all the effort."

"So do you think Felicia made the right choice when she married Rudy?" Marcie asked.

"She was pretty convincing that afternoon. I could see myself agreeing with her, and for a while I thought she'd made the right choice. They got married right out of high school, back in 1936. Three years later Seldon was born. Quentin let everyone know that Rudy was officially running the farm, although no one really believed that Rudy could run himself, let alone the farm. Quentin and Rebecca fixed up the attic and moved up there. Felicia, Rudy, and Sel had the second floor."

Marcie was pleased to hear that the guesses she and Kevin had made about the layout of the house were accurate.

"I visited her there quite a few times back in those days, when I was home from school. Things seemed to be working out for her. I mean, it wasn't perfect. Rudy was still Rudy. But she got along real well with Rebecca. Rebecca was like a second, and a better, mother to her. And Felicia seemed to adore little Sel."

"What went wrong?" Marcie asked.

Ellen shrugged. "A lot of things, I guess. The first was that Rebecca got cancer and died a year or so after Sel was born. Nothing was the same after that. Quentin started having these wild mood swings. One day he'd hardly speak, then the next day he would be gabbing away a mile a minute. When he was down, he'd take it out on Rudy and Felicia. She told me she even had to keep Sel out of the way of his grandfather on those days. That was when she started standing up to Quentin, to protect little Sel."

"Had Quentin always been that way?"

"He'd always been this larger-than-life kind of guy. It was almost as if he was trying to make up for only having one arm. He loved to argue with the men and show how charming he could be with the women. It could get annoying at times, but everyone felt a little sorry for him and made allowances. Plus, Rebecca always made sure he didn't go too far. She'd just give him a look if he was getting too boisterous, and Quentin would calm down."

"So without her, Quentin spun out of control?" Marcie asked.

"That's when it started, anyway. Then came the war. Rudy got drafted pretty early on, and that left Felicia and Quentin living there with the boy. For all that Quentin made fun of his son—and he could really put the needle in, if you know what I mean—I think he loved him deeply." The woman paused. "Felicia once told me that if Rudy had been smart, Quentin might have hated him because he would have had brains and beauty both. But Felicia said that in a way Quentin thought of his son as the other half of himself. Quentin had the brains but a mutilated body, while Rudy was just the opposite. They were the two sides of the same coin."

"And it was about three years after Rudy went into the army that those men were murdered in the barn," Marcie said.

"That's right."

"I saw Sel the day he died, and he said he had solid evidence as to who committed that crime. I've looked into what went on back then, and it seems to me that the three victims were all pretty unpopular in town because they had done things that hurt people serving in the war. Heller ran over the Campbell boy, and Carter and Fuller supposedly worked together to cheat Mrs. Proctor out of her farm while her husband was serving."

Ellen Barkum nodded. "Those were all sad events. The Campbell boy's death was an accident. Had Jake been drinking before it happened? I imagine so. Lots of men stopped by for a few beers before heading home in those days. Still do, I suppose. But we all knew that Joe didn't always look where he was going when he was on that bike. Everyone would have just sighed and moved on, except that his father was killed in Europe."

"What about the Proctors?" Marcie persisted.

"Simon Proctor was a handsome, bright, and ambitious man. But he was young, and when he inherited the farm, he figured that he could do just about everything better than his daddy did. So he hurried out and bought a lot of new equipment on credit and figured that he was smart enough to make the money to pay for it. Maybe he would have, if nothing had gone wrong, but in farming something almost always goes wrong. Even if he hadn't been away in the Army, I don't think things would have turned out much differently."

"But George Fuller and Matt Carter did take advantage of Proctor's bad luck," Marcie said.

The older woman shrugged. "That's the way of the world. If they hadn't grabbed it, somebody else would have. Some of those folks who said all those bad things about Fuller and Carter after Simon Proctor got killed would have been quick enough to snatch up that farm if those boys hadn't gotten there first."

"From some of the things that Sel said shortly before he died, I got the idea that he thought his grandfather might have been involved in those murders. Do you think that's possible?"

Ellen Barkum jumped to her feet. "I'm going to make a pot of coffee. Would you like some?"

Before Marcie could answer, the woman left the room.

Chapter Fourteen

Kevin knew that the woman who answered the door wasn't Elaine Page, Joe Campbell's sister, because she would have to be in her early seventies, while the woman in front of him was only in her forties. Slim with dark hair, she gave the impression of calm efficiency.

"You must be the reporter here to see my mother," she said with a wary smile, before he could introduce himself. "I'm Maggie Carson. Mom is sitting out back on the screened porch."

The woman closed the door behind him, then turned and walked quickly toward the rear of the house. Kevin followed her, getting only a vague impression of a tidy, uncluttered living room.

"The reporter is here to see you," the woman announced, taking a step down into a room with floor-to-ceiling screens.

A plump woman with a large amount of carefully

arranged gray hair was sitting alone at one end of the porch. A magazine was in her lap, and next to her, leaning against the arm of the chair, was a metal cane with three rubber-tipped prongs on the end. Kevin went over and introduced himself, and the woman's face lit up in a smile. She motioned for Kevin to sit in the rattan chair across from her.

"Are you sure you don't need anything right now, Mom?" her daughter asked, perhaps hoping that her mother would ask her to sit in on the interview.

"No, thank you, dear, I think I'm all set," she replied. After waiting for her daughter to leave the room, she turned to Kevin. "I'm very pleased that you're going to write something for the newspaper about my brother, Joe. When someone dies young like that, they sort of fall off the map. Even in the family, lots of the younger people don't even know that he ever existed. There aren't many people left in town who remember the accident."

"No, I guess not. My article is going to be a general piece discussing all the events leading up to the hangings at the Hayes farm. Sel Hayes' death has made all that news again."

"I was only a child when those three men died. I was too young to be aware of it at the time, but I guess from what my mother told me later on, some people thought there was a connection between Joe's death and the murder of those men."

"Did your mother believe that?"

"She didn't talk about it much. You have to remember she had a lot on her plate at the time. My father was killed a few months after Joe, and she had to spend most of her time working to make ends meet. I don't think she had enough energy left at the end of the day to speculate on the murder of those men. But even if she'd had the time, I doubt that she would have thought about it. She was a very practical, down-to-earth type of woman. She didn't believe in wasting time speculating about things you couldn't change." Elaine Page leaned forward in her chair and spoke in a whisper. "My daughter reminds me a lot of her. She's a computer whiz. Everything she reads is about computers."

Kevin gave her a conspiratorial smile. "But you're different?"

She picked up a large paperback from the table beside her. "I read novels," she said proudly. "Mysteries, romances, even horror."

"Then maybe you can tell me the story about what happened at the time your brother was killed."

The woman looked across the porch and out toward the bird feeder in the middle of the backyard, where a noisy blue jay was chasing the smaller birds away.

"I don't remember very much. You have to realize that I was very young then. I was six when Dad died, so I was only five when Joe got hit."

"How old was your brother?"

"Eight. Oh, and was he a wild one. My mother had all she could do to manage him. Took after his father, she always said." The woman paused. "That might be another reason she never talked about it much. I think she always blamed herself for not keeping a closer eye on Joe. But she worked down at the hardware store afternoons until five. The next-door neighbor, Mrs. Putney, looked after me and Joe along with her own children until Mom came home. But Joe was always off somewhere on that bike of his. Mom knew because Mrs. Putney told her, but there wasn't much she could do. Telling Joe to behave was like trying to tame the wind."

Kevin nodded. "I know it's probably painful, even now, but can you tell me what you remember about the day that Joe died?"

"A police office knocked on Mrs. Putney's door. They talked outside, and then he went off in the direction of what I later figured must have been the hardware store. When Mrs. Putney came back inside, I could see she'd been crying and looked scared. I guess she figured that Mom would blame her for what happened to Joe. Although I have to say, Mom never did hold her responsible. Mrs. Putney told us to play quietly. That something had happened to Joe, and Mom would be coming to get me soon. I knew right away that Joe was dead. When things *happened to people,* it was never good."

"Did your mother come to get you?"

"Yes. But it was a long time later, after dark. Mrs. Putney gave me supper. Mom came by and spoke to Mrs. Putney alone for a few minutes in the other room. Then she took me home. I kept looking to see if she was upset, but except for walking a little stiffer than usual and rushing me along, you'd never have known that Joe had just been killed. When we got home, we sat at the kitchen table. She warmed up a little milk for me, then told me that my brother was dead. She said, 'Now there's just the two of us until your father comes home.' Of course, six months later, he was killed too."

"Did your mother ever say anything about Jake Heller, the man who hit your brother?"

"Just that he was drunk. And Mom said the word *drunk* like it was something really disgusting. That stayed with me a long time. I guess it's part of the reason I've never taken a drink."

"Did she ever say anything about people wanting to punish Heller for what he did?"

"Like I said, Mom never talked about it at all. I think she felt too guilty to blame anyone else. I don't know what my father wrote back to her when she sent him a letter telling him what happened. But I always had a feeling that when my father died, Mom was sort of relieved, because she'd never have been able to face him."

"How about the rest of your family? Did they say or do anything?"

"My father was an only child, and his parents lived in New Hampshire. We never saw them again after Dad's funeral. Mom's parents and her brother lived up north. We hardly ever saw them either. She always told me that we couldn't expect anything from them, and that blood wasn't always thicker than water."

"What about neighbors or friends? Did they visit?"

"The only person I can remember coming around to see us was the chief of police, Mr. McDermott."

"When was that?"

"I guess it was a week or so after Joe was killed. He came to our house and talked to my mother for a while. Then he came into my bedroom where I was playing and talked to me."

"What did he say?"

Glen Ebisch

"I remember that he spoke to me like I was an adult. He was a really big man, and he got right down on the floor and talked to me like it was the most normal thing in the world. He told me he was sorry that my brother was dead. He said that if I ever needed any help, I should get in touch with him." Mrs. Page smiled. "I remember telling him very solemnly that I thought my mother and I would get along just fine. He smiled at me when I said that and patted my head."

"Did he say anything else?"

"Only that losing a brother was a very hard thing. I re-member his saying that because it came as a surprise to me. Joe was older than me, and he was a boy, so we hardly ever did things together. I didn't think much was going to change in my life just because Joe was gone un-til the chief said that." Mrs. Page looked down at her lap and shook her head. "The other reason I remember it is because that was the first time I had seen a grown man cry."

Chapter Fifteen

Mrs. Barkum came back into the living room carrying a tray with two cups of coffee, cream, and sugar and a plate of what looked to Marcie like store-bought cookies.

"Sorry about the cookies," the woman said, as if reading her mind. "I never have been much for baking. In fact, cooking in general has always been pretty much of a mystery to me. George did most of that—another little way in which we were different from the rest of the town. I did most of the yard work, while he puttered around in the kitchen."

Marcie smiled. "Sounds like you were a very contemporary couple."

A shadow passed over the woman's face. "We bumped along pretty well together, I suppose."

Marcie sipped her coffee and ate a cookie. She figured this was one of those times where, as Greg said, you had to give the person a chance to work up enough strength to answer. Mrs. Barkum would either find that strength or she wouldn't, but for Marcie to press her on it would just make her answering less likely.

"You were asking me whether Quentin Hayes could have had anything to do with those hangings," the woman finally said, putting down her cup.

Marcie nodded cautiously.

"Things got kind of complicated out at the Hayes farm after Rudy went away. There were just the three of them left: Quentin, Felicia, and Sel. I didn't get to see Felicia all that often after that because I was away in Burlington at college, and I started staying there in the summer to work. But I remember running into Felicia in the general store over Christmas. It must have been the Christmas of forty-three, because those murders hadn't happened yet."

"What did she say?" Marcie asked.

Ellen Barkum sighed. "Felicia was having some trouble with Quentin. Living out there all alone and with Rebecca and Rudy gone, I guess he started to take a romantic interest in her. Like I said, she was a very attractive girl."

"But he must have been more than thirty years older than she was," Marcie said, horrified. "And he only had one arm."

"I'm afraid that Quentin was the sort of man who thought that he'd be charming to women even if he had no arms. I asked Felicia how bad it was, and she said it wasn't anything that she couldn't handle."

"She should have called the police," Marcie said in a tone of outrage.

Mrs. Barkum smiled. "In those days you didn't go to the police about things like that. Families worked it out for themselves."

"But Felicia didn't have anyone," Marcie said. "Her father and mother didn't want any more to do with her, and with Rudy away, there wasn't anyone she could turn to."

"That wasn't entirely true."

"What do you mean?"

"George Fuller went to high school with us. George was a good-looking guy and full of fun, and he went out with lots of girls both in school and afterward. But he'd always been especially attracted to Felicia. Even in high school I think that Felicia sometimes thought about dropping Rudy for George. He certainly had more brains. But she was always afraid that George would run off with another girl at the first opportunity. One thing about Rudy, he was as faithful as a good dog."

"But when Quentin started bothering her, she turned to George?" asked Marcie.

Mrs. Barkum nodded. "She kept real quiet about it. As you can imagine, folks in town didn't exactly approve of a woman cheating on her husband when he was away fighting in the war. I only know because she told me that Easter when I came home for a visit. She wanted me to know that she was only doing it because of Quentin's misbehaving."

"What happened?"

"She told me that George came around one night and told Quentin in no uncertain terms that if he so much as touched Felicia, George would see that he didn't have the use of his other arm for a long time. Felicia said that Quentin was furious, but there wasn't much he could do. George was a big fellow, and although he seemed easygoing most of the time, he was known to have quite a temper."

"Were things all right after that?"

"Yes and no. Quentin left her alone. Felicia said that he pretty much stayed up in the attic when he was in the house. Otherwise he spent most of his time working on the farm. Spring is a busy time, and they had lots of un-skilled help that needed to be supervised."

"So what was the problem?"

"I think Felicia got to thinking that maybe she'd made the wrong decision by marrying Rudy. Maybe if she'd never gotten involved with George, she'd have stayed happily married to Rudy for fifty years if he had lived—although I doubt it. But I think she got the idea in her head that she could divorce Rudy and go off with George to start over again."

"Did she actually tell you that?"

"When I talked to her about a month before the hang-ings, she said that it was something she was thinking about."

"Do you think Quentin knew?"

"He must have considered the possibility. After all, he knew Rudy's limitations, and he had to suspect that a woman like Felicia might have bigger plans than spend-ing her life on a hardscrabble farm."

Marcie sat back in her chair and studied the lava lamp on the corner table.

"Did Felicia think that Quentin helped in the hanging of those men in order to get rid of George?"

"At first she suspected it, but as time went by, she became more and more convinced of it. I only saw her a couple of times after the hangings, but there was no doubt in her mind that Quentin had been involved in the killings. It tore her up that there was no way she could prove it. But in her own way she got revenge."

"How's that?"

Mrs. Barkum smiled. "By seeing ghosts. A few months after the murders, Felicia suddenly began seeing ghosts out in the barn. And I guess she could be pretty convincing in telling people about them, because it got harder and harder for Quentin to hire help. There were a lot more jobs than available workers in those days. So once that story started going around, people would say that although they didn't personally believe in ghosts, why not work at another farm where you didn't even have to wonder about it? Before long it was a real struggle for Quentin to keep the place going. He put Sel to work when he was real young and managed to find a few workers to help him barely scrape along."

"So you don't think Felicia ever really saw any ghosts?"

The woman gave Marcie an odd look. "Funny you should ask that. The last time I saw her I asked the same question. She admitted that at first they were just stories she made up to get back at Quentin. But then she said that one evening when she was in the barn, she heard voices. At first she thought that it was some of the hired men hanging around late talking, but then she recognized one of the voices as George Fuller's. She went back night after night, and before long she heard all three voices: Jake, George, and Matt's. They always spoke the same words. Felicia figured that it was the last conversation they'd had before they died." Mrs. Barkum paused. "I don't believe in ghosts, but Felicia seemed sure."

"Did she know who had murdered the men?"

"I think she did by the way she looked at me when I asked. But Felicia wouldn't come right out and tell me. If I'd gotten to see her again, I might have been able to find out. But she hardly ever left the house after the hangings. She'd cook and clean and take care of Sel, but she wouldn't lift a hand to do more. Of course, she didn't stay around very long. About a year after the hangings she disappeared. Everyone figured that she had been waiting for Rudy to get back, and when word came that he'd been killed, she decided to take off."

"But she left her son."

The woman nodded. "I think a lot of folks in town would have been more sympathetic to her leaving if she'd taken Sel along. Most folks knew that Quentin was getting odder with every passing year and wouldn't have blamed her except for that. I guess they were kind of shocked. I wasn't."

"Why not?"

"An attractive widow by herself has a lot better chance of making a new start than one with a child. Felicia always took care of the boy, but I think eventually he reminded her too much of the mistake she'd made when she married his father."

"Did you ever her from her again?"

She shook her head. "But I never really expected to. Felicia didn't fit in here, and I'm sure once she left, she had no desire to look back."

Marcie glanced around at the room's furnishings. "You never really fit in either."

Mrs. Barkum smiled. "And I was happy living up in Burlington until I came home one summer for a visit and met my George. That's the only reason I moved back here."

"Felicia met her George too, but he was taken away from her."

"And if he hadn't been murdered, maybe after Rudy was killed, Felicia and George would have married and settled down right here." A look of fierce longing passed over Ellen Barkum's face. "It would have been nice to have had a friend all these years."

Chapter Sixteen

Marcie drove out of Ellen Barkum's little neighborhood of 1950s homes and kept going until she found a spot by the side of the road wide enough for her to pull over. It was time to try to piece together what she had learned so far. Bits and pieces of ideas were floating around in her mind, begging for some kind of rational organization.

She turned off the engine and looked across the meadow that ran from the road to the tree line. In the distance, hills covered in the light green of late spring gave the scene the kind of picture-postcard quality that fooled urban dwellers into thinking that nothing bad ever happened in the country. Taking deep breaths, she forced her mind to slow, an old yoga technique. When she felt reasonably relaxed, Marcie began to examine the evidence.

One question had clearly been answered. She had wondered why Quentin Hayes would have gotten in-

volved in the plot to kill the three men. At first she had
thought it was because his son had died in the war, but
Rudy's death occurred after the murders had taken place,
so that didn't make sense. Ellen Barkum's information about the relationship between Felicia and George
Fuller, however, had provided the answer. Quentin would
have resented George's involvement with Felicia because it prevented him from continuing to sexually ha-
rass her. And he even might have felt that George had
tempted Felicia into being unfaithful to Rudy. Both
would have been reasons for him to provide his barn as
the place for the crimes. He might not have cared about
the other two men, but eliminating George was clearly a
priority to him.

Another question to which Marcie thought she now
had the answer concerned what Sel had learned from
his grandfather's papers that motivated him to say that
he would have liked to push his grandfather down the
stairs. If Quentin's papers had revealed his campaign
of sexual harassment toward Felicia, then once Sel
read them, he might well have felt anger and bitterness
toward his grandfather. However, that raised another
question that had been bothering Marcie since the beginning: why would Quentin have kept a written record of
his activities? It wasn't exactly the sort of thing that a
grandfather would be proud to pass on to his grandson—
or to anyone else, for that matter.

A thread of an idea took shape in Marcie's mind.
Quentin had obviously not intended for Sel or anyone
else to find those papers implicating him in the hangings.
He had, after all, concealed them behind a wall. So what

had been his purpose in keeping written evidence of his crimes?

Like grandfather, like grandson, Marcie suddenly thought. Perhaps Quentin had been trying to blackmail the other person who was involved in the hangings. The person who had actually strung up the three men while Quentin and Sel were out fishing in the creek. Possibly he wrote down the complete story of what had happened as a way of protecting himself from his blackmail victim— don't think of killing me because that will guarantee that all the evidence against you comes out.

Marcie's mind took another leap. What if Quentin's threat hadn't worked? Was it possible, then, that his fall down the stairs wasn't an accident at all, but a case of his accomplice's eliminating a blackmail threat? It would be interesting to know more about the circumstances surrounding Quentin's death. Maybe that way she'd find a clue as to who had actually committed those murders over sixty years ago. And that, in turn, would lead to the solution of the more recent murder.

Kevin had gotten what little information he had about Quentin's death by talking to Jack Brill at The Lonesome Pine, so maybe a visit there would be worthwhile. Marcie had passed the bar a couple of times on her travels around Doric, so she started the engine and headed off in that direction.

Kevin drove past the statehouse in downtown Montpelier. He went two blocks, then made a left and pulled into the small parking lot behind a stone building that looked a lot like a small bank but was actually the home of the

Courier. It looked like a bank because it had originally been built for that purpose, but Kevin's grandfather had purchased it after the bank went belly up during the Depression. Kevin's father was proud of the building because, as he often pointed out on public occasions, he thought it showed the importance of journalism as one of the foundation stones of democracy. Kevin thought, less generously, that the building's lack of a modern heating and air-conditioning system and its general atmosphere of chilly dampness made it a particularly unpleasant place to work.

That thought was on his mind at the moment because he was in the newspaper's basement, where old editions were kept. Even though a dehumidifier was groaning away in the background, supposedly maintaining appropriately dry conditions, Kevin thought a clammy dankness permeated the air. Real reporters usually got interns to do this kind of background research, but as a stringer he didn't merit that kind of assistance, and, in fact, he wasn't sure that he wanted others at the paper to know the details of the story he was working on. Just as in any other office, word got around quickly whenever anything out of the routine was taking place. And the story of the hanging men was anything but routine.

Kevin had finished his work and come upstairs to the main floor when, as luck would have it, he bumped into his father coming through the impressive brass front doors.

"Kevin, can I talk to you for a minute?" Not waiting to receive a response, his father kept walking through the first-floor newsroom, nodding absentmindedly to his employees, and got into the elevator to the second floor, where he occupied a corner office.

Kevin got into the elevator with him. "How are you and Mom doing?" Kevin asked as the old elevator wheezed its way upward.

"Your mother is fine, although she is wondering why we've only seen you once this week even though you're supposedly living in our house."

"I've been following up on a story."

"So I've heard. That's what I want to talk to you about."

Nothing more was said as the elevator came to a halt. Kevin matched his father stride for stride down the marble hall to his office. His father nodded to his secretary, who gave Kevin a brief, sympathetic glance; then he marched into his office and sat behind his desk. He motioned Kevin into the chair on the other side and began going through his mail.

"I had a call from Chief Roylston yesterday," he said, opening a thick envelope. "He told me that you've gotten involved in an ongoing homicide investigation into the death of Seldon Hayes. It seems that the chief is concerned that you might jeopardize his investigation and possibly put yourself at some risk."

"I think the chief is more concerned that I might get to the bottom of the whole thing," Kevin said.

"What's that supposed to mean?"

"The death of Sel Hayes is connected to the three men who were hanged in his barn back in 1944, a crime Doric has been happy to keep hidden away. So let's just say that I don't think the chief is very eager to have that all raked up again. He'd be just as happy to bury the Sel Hayes case and pass it off as a suicide."

"Are you sure it isn't?"

Kevin paused, knowing that it was never wise to claim to know more than one did when talking to his father.

"I'm not positive. But I think it's very likely he was murdered. And it should be clear once the autopsy report is completed. I think it will show that Hayes was heavily sedated at the time of his death, just like those three men hanged sixty years ago."

"Surely you don't think it's the same killer, do you? He'd be an old man by now."

Kevin blushed, recalling that Marcie had made the same point.

"Probably not the same person. But the killer has to be somebody who wants to hide what really happened back then."

"However, you don't know who either of these killers might be, am I right?"

Kevin gripped the arms of the chair more tightly. His hands often started to shake when he was dealing with one of his father's interrogations, and to reveal that would be a sign of weakness.

"Not yet. But I'm reasonably certain that Sel Hayes had evidence as to the identity of the original killer, and knowing who that person is will lead us to the person who killed Sel."

"But you haven't found that evidence."

"No. But—"

"Is it likely that you will find that evidence in the near future?" his father interrupted.

"It's too early to tell. I've only been working on the story for a couple of days." Kevin could feel that he was losing the argument. "And this is an important story, despite what Chief Roylston says."

His father put down the mail and gave Kevin a searching look. "Since you have refused to become an official member of the *Courier* team and continue to remain a freelancer, I can't officially demand that you give up this investigation. But I would hope that as my son you would have the courtesy to listen to my concerns. Will you do that?"

Kevin nodded reluctantly, pretty sure he wouldn't like what he was going to hear.

"This is a regional newspaper, and as such we have to maintain a cordial relationship with local businesses and municipal authorities. We depend on the businesses for our advertising, and on the local authorities for access to information. If we offend our advertisers, we go out of business. If we offend local officials, we find that local television and radio stations are getting the stories before we do. That's why I take what Chief Roylston says seriously. Do you understand?"

Kevin's fingers pressed into the arms of the chair, and he nodded. "But does that mean we ignore important stories because they might offend local officials who aren't doing their jobs?"

"Of course not," his father snapped. "But in the absence of any hard evidence, all you're doing is engaging in a fishing expedition that is likely to antagonize people without resulting in any significant evidence. And although I can't order you to stop, I can stop the paper from printing any more of your pieces until you come to your senses."

"You'd do that?" Kevin asked.

His father sighed. "I think it's time you made a decision as to whether you seriously want to be a journalist. This half-in, half-out approach you've been taking is simply delaying the inevitable, and I'm afraid that I've been responsible for enabling you to continue this way. You have to decide whether you want to be a journalist or whether you want to pursue another kind of career."

Kevin got to his feet, his face red with anger. "That's what this is all about, isn't it? You want to keep me under your thumb. Well, I'm going to keep working on this story whether the *Courier* publishes it or not." He turned and walked stiffly toward the door.

"Kevin."

When he turned to look back, his father was standing behind his desk. Instead of the anger he expected to see on his father's face, he saw concern.

"I'm only trying to do what I think is best for you. But if you feel that you have to pursue this story, please be careful. We'll talk again when you've gotten over this obsession."

Kevin gave his father a curt nod and left.

Chapter Seventeen

Marcie took a deep breath and pushed open the door of The Lonesome Pine. As she walked inside, she could tell from the discolored knotty pine and the pungent smell of disinfectant that this was the kind of bar usually occupied by men rather than women. It was still early, only about 3:30, so most of the customers were likely still at work. That probably accounted for the small group of three or four guys who were huddled at the far end of the bar with beers in front of them and their eyes fixed on the television. They turned in unison and gave her an appraising glance. When she ignored them, their attention slowly drifted back to the baseball game they were watching. It reminded her of the few times that she had gone to the NCO club as a guest of her father. Even though there were plenty of female noncommissioned officers by then, the atmosphere was still highly charged with testosterone. Only women who had fully convinced themselves that they were one of the guys felt comfortable there. She suspected the same was true of The Lonesome Pine.

The bartender, a man with bushy black hair, broke away from the group and came in her direction. He gave Marcie a long look, as if surprised to see someone of her gender and age in the place at that time of day.

"What can I get you?"

"Are you Jack Brill?"

The man gave a reluctant nod.

"I'm Marcie Ducasse, a friend of Kevin Murray. I'd like to ask you a few questions."

"You'll have to order something."

"Let me have a club soda with a twist of lime."

"If I get any more hard drinkers like you and Kevin, I'll go out of business," Jack said with a thin smile.

"It's a little early in the day for me," she said.

Jack's glance slid to the end of the bar. "Fortunately, not for some." He walked away. A minute later he returned and put the glass down in front of her. He took her money, and when he brought back the change, he said, "What do you want to know?"

"I believe you told Kevin that Sel's grandfather, Quentin Hayes, died by falling down the stairs in the farmhouse."

Jack thought for a moment. "Yeah, that's the story that Sel was telling people here one night a few months ago when he was feeling sorry for himself. He said that his father was killed in the war, his mother ran away and left him a few months later, then—I think he said it was about ten years later—his grandfather fell down the stairs and died. That was right about when he turned seventeen, I guess."

"What happened after his grandfather died?"

"The farm had been going downhill pretty steadily ever since the war. Sel and his grandfather and a few hands they hired when things were busy were doing all the work. But I gathered that things had gotten bad. So once his grandfather died, Sel went to work in a factory up near Montpelier. But he kept living on the farm."

"Then he got married."

"Yeah. Somewhere along the way after that he got married, but I'm not sure exactly when."

"Did Sel say anything more specific about the details of his grandfather's death?"

"I think he said that his grandfather had sent him into town to buy some feed for the few animals they still had. He was only gone about forty minutes, and when he got back, he found the old man's body crumpled up at the bottom of the stairs that came down from the attic."

Marcie sipped her club soda. "Did Sel give any indication that he thought it was anything other than an accident?"

Jack's eyes widened in surprise. "He told me that the drawers in his grandfather's upstairs dresser were pulled open. He thought that Quentin had been looking for something. Then for some reason he started hurrying downstairs, tripped, and fell. He only had one arm, you know."

"But he'd been up and down those stairs hundreds of times."

"And this time he stepped the wrong way and lost his

balance. That's why they call them accidents. I guess the police saw it the same way."

"Sel only started talking a few months ago about having evidence of who killed the hanging men?"

"Right. I told Kevin all about that."

"Did Sel say anything about where he might have been keeping that evidence?"

"I don't remember his ever saying. Like I told Kevin, when guys asked him questions about it, he got real quiet. He even acted a little scared, as if he didn't want anyone to know what he'd found out." Jack smiled. "That was Sel's problem. He was always real careful when he was sober, but once he got a few drinks under his belt, he'd run off at the mouth like crazy. You couldn't shut him up."

"But he never gave away where this evidence might have been hidden?"

"The most I can remember is one night a couple of guys were teasing him about how he should get a safe deposit box to keep these important documents. And Sel got this real sly look on his face and said that they shouldn't worry because he'd hidden the stuff real well. He said that he had them in a place that belonged to the devil, whatever that was supposed to mean."

"Were those his exact words?" Marcie asked.

Jack frowned. "It's been a month or more now. But I think that's what he said. I've got a real good memory when it comes to conversations, and you've got to admit that was an odd thing to say."

"Okay." Marcie got up from her stool. "Thanks for your help."

"Sure. And when you see Kevin, tell him that you

talked to me, and that he can add this conversation to my bill."

The men at the far end of the bar all turned to stare at Marcie when she left The Lonesome Pine. She went out to her car and sat there for a moment with the window open, listening to the hum of the occasional car that passed and enjoying the aroma of the plants in the open field. It was possible that Quentin Hayes had been black-mailing his murderous partner and been killed for his efforts. After all, the farm was doing badly, so it was possible that ten years after the crime he decided to try to cash in on what he knew. Maybe Quentin figured that his involvement was so peripheral that he could threaten to go to the police. He probably figured he could claim that he simply provided the barn as a meeting place, never imagining that it would lead to three men being hanged.

Marcie suddenly realized that she was sitting all alone out in the middle of an exposed parking lot in Doric, which was not the safest thing to do, given the threatening note she had received. Her thoughts stopped short. Why would Sel's killer be threatening her if he already had Quentin Hayes' papers? Why would he care if she stayed in town if the evidence had already been destroyed? Maybe, Marcie thought, just maybe that meant Quentin's papers were still out there somewhere.

Jack had just told her that Sel claimed the papers were in a place the belonged to the devil. She suddenly re-called how Sel had stood under the beam in the barn and declared that to be the devil's place. Marcie called Kevin from her cell phone.

"Where are you?" she asked, when he finally answered in a mumble.

"In Montpelier."

"What are you doing there?"

"Eating ice cream."

"Well, it's good to know that one of us is working hard on this story."

"I just had a big fight with my dad, so I thought I'd get some ice cream to boost my spirits. We got into an argument over this story. He kept saying that I didn't have any evidence. I told him that I was going to keep working on this story until I got some, but you know, Marcie, I really have no idea what to do next. I've really got nothing but suspicions."

"I might have a cure for that, but you'll have to meet me at the Hayes farm."

"We don't have the keys to the house. I returned them to Steve McDermott when we finished our search yesterday."

"That's okay. We're not going to go into the house. We're going to check out the barn."

"It'll take us days to find anything in there."

"I'm hoping that I can narrow it down. How long will it take you to get there?"

"Forty minutes."

"Okay, I'll see you out at the farm."

Marcie drove back through town, relieved to see that in her various travels through Doric she had been right in thinking that there was a small hardware store just past the center of town. She pulled into a lot that already held two pickup trucks, one pulling a horse trailer, and went into the store. An elderly man stood behind the counter chatting with a man only slightly younger who was wearing overalls and a cap with a truck logo on it. They stopped talking as she walked up to the counter, and they looked at her with amused expressions.

"Can I help you, miss?" the man behind the counter asked.

"Where do you have crowbars?"

"Now, what would you want a crowbar for?" the other man asked before she got an answer.

"Demolition," Marcie said coolly, keeping her eyes on the man behind the counter and ignoring his friend.

"What would *you* want to demolish?" the man persisted.

Marcie slowly turned to look at him. "Whatever gets in my way."

The man held Marcie's eyes for a second; then his glance shifted to the floor.

"We have crowbars right down aisle three," the man behind the counter said nervously, pointing toward the rear of the store.

"Thanks."

Marcie discovered that they came in two-foot and three-foot lengths. Although she was tempted to buy the three-footer just to show her friend up front that she could handle it, the longer one was heavy and more awkward to use. So she went with the two-foot length. She carried it back to the front of the store and plunked it down on the counter where the two men were still talking. The man behind the counter rang up the sale without comment.

"Good luck on your project," the other man said as she headed for the door.

Marcie didn't detect any sarcasm, so she turned back and smiled. "Thanks. I may need it."

Chapter Eighteen

Pulling out of the parking lot, Marcie turned north and headed toward the Hayes farm. She was hoping that Kevin would drive fast, because she would be at the farm in fifteen minutes and didn't care for the idea of being there alone any longer than she had to be.

The ride down the narrow lane to the farm seemed so familiar that it was hard to believe that she had made it for the first time only three days ago. When Marcie reached the farmyard, she stopped the car and looked carefully for any signs that there was anyone else around. There were no vehicles other than Sel's broken-down truck, which still sat forlornly by the side of the barn, and no signs of life.

Marcie got out of the car. She grabbed her flashlight and the crowbar from the floor in the back. Feeling around under the front seat, she discovered a pair of work gloves that she carried in case of roadside emergencies.

They'd help her do battle with the barn doors that Kevin and Steve had closed after they searched the barn yesterday. She decided to stand by the car until Kevin arrived. Being near her vehicle was reassuring in the desolate farmyard. She was looking in the direction of the barn when the farmhouse door slammed behind her. She spun around, her heart jumping into her throat.

"Marcie, what are you doing out here?" Steve McDermott asked, smiling as he came down off the porch. He was wearing an open-necked knit shirt and jeans. He looked younger than he had in a suit, and even more attractive.

"Hi, Steve, what are you doing here?" Marcie stammered, her mind racing to come up with a plausible excuse for trespassing. "I didn't see your car."

"I'm parked in back of the house. I figured that I'd have a final look around to make sure I hadn't missed any important papers that I'll need to settle Sel's estate." He pulled at the fabric of his shirt with two fingers. "I thought that I'd better dress down, considering that Sel wasn't much of a housekeeper."

He stood there smiling at her, waiting for her to answer the same question. As Steve's glance took in the work gloves and the crowbar, Marcie knew that her options had narrowed pretty much to telling the truth. The worst he could do was order her off the property. Then she'd go back to the road to wait for Kevin and tell him that she'd messed up their one chance to solve the case.

"I had an idea about where Sel might have hidden some papers he got from his grandfather. Papers that might tell us who hanged those men in the barn."

Steve's eyes widened. "Really? You mean there might be some actual evidence that will put the case to rest? That would be great. Where do we have to go?"

"To the barn, I think."

"Why there?"

"Sel told someone that he'd put the evidence in the 'devil's place,' and that's how I heard him talk about the spot where the men were hanged. I figured that maybe he hid the evidence somewhere in there."

Steve's brow wrinkled.

"I know it's kind of thin."

"But it's worth a try," Steve said. "Why don't we have a look around?"

"Kevin should be coming along in a few minutes."

"Good. We'll need all the help we can find to search around in there. It's a mess."

He led the way across the yard, and between the two of them they were able to pull open the doors to the barn. Once inside, Marcie turned on her flashlight and guided them through the obstructions to the back. She stopped in her tracks and shuddered for a moment when she saw that the rope was still hanging down from the rafter, right where they had left it. Obviously Chief Roylston hadn't considered the matter important enough to even send someone out to retrieve the rope. It swung back and forth hypnotically in the gentle breeze.

"I guess the chief thought that since it was kids playing a prank, there was no reason to make taking it down a priority," McDermott said, reading her mind.

"Yeah, it looks that way."

There was enough light coming between the boards

and through the open doors that when Marcie turned off the flashlight, they could still see well enough to work.

"Why don't we start right under the beam?" Steve suggested, "We can work out from there."

They began by carefully clearing away the piles of hay with an old pitchfork and removing the pieces of equipment that were scattered about on the floor. They worked carefully, going out about four feet in both directions from center, but found nothing.

Marcie stood and stared up for a moment at the beam from which the men had been hanged. She tried to reconstruct how the crime had been committed. Her mind drifted back to the summer afternoon over sixty years ago. She could picture the four men—the three victims and their killer—gathered in the barn on the pretext of discussing something. What the ploy had been to get them here in the first place, she didn't know. Then their killer had suggested that they have a drink, maybe to celebrate their future business endeavor.

Once the three victims were semiconscious, the fourth man had carried them one at a time up into the hayloft. He'd probably already prepared the nooses. Then he fitted one around each of their necks in turn, tied the rope in place, and shoved them off the end of the loft. She could almost hear the snap of the rope as it pulled taut with the sudden weight of each body.

"Are you okay, Marcie?" Steve asked, his expression worried.

She smiled. "Yeah, I'm fine.

"We should finish cleaning up around here," Steve suggested.

Marcie took an old broom that was in one of the stalls and carefully swept the area they had cleared, revealing the rough wood flooring. Using the flashlight, Steve began to carefully examine each of the boards. The wood was distressed from years of hooves, wagon wheels, and pitchforks, but Steve thought that a couple of the boards showed signs of being recently hammered back into place.

He fitted the crowbar under the end of one and tried to pry the board up. It was dense, hard wood, and it took a lot of effort to get the one end to slowly come up an inch from the frame under it. He shifted the bar to the other end of the board and began pushing again.

"What are you doing?" a voice asked.

The bar slipped, and Steve sprawled forward. Marcie looked up. All she saw was the eye of a flashlight focused on her. The beam dropped, and Kevin walked toward them.

"Don't you make any noise? Couldn't you say 'hello' or something?" she said.

"Hello. Sorry I scared you. I'm surprised to see you here, Steve." The coldness in Kevin's voice was obvious.

Steve scrambled back up into a crouch. "I happened to be here and decided to give Marcie a hand."

"So I see. What are you two doing?" Kevin asked again, coming closer. He paused when he saw the noose hanging down from the rafter but didn't comment. He quickly redirected his flashlight to the floorboards.

"I'm trying to get a few of these boards up to see if

anything is under the floor," Steve said. "Do you want to give it a try?"

Kevin took the crowbar, clearly happy to take charge. "You think Sel hid his grandfather's papers under here?"

"I think that in Sel's mind, anyway, this would be the last place that anybody would look," Marcie answered.

"It's certainly the last place that I would look," Kevin grunted, now down on his knees and pushing hard on the crowbar.

After several more minutes of effort at both ends, the board was worked loose. The nails squealed as Kevin pulled it out.

"Let me have the flashlight," he said. He shined the light into the three-inch wide crack and peered into the space. Soon he was down on his belly, trying to get a better look.

"Do you see something?" asked Marcie.

"A piece of plastic, I think."

"Somebody must have put it there," Marcie said with excitement. "They sure didn't have plastic when this barn was built. Can you reach it?"

Kevin stuck his hand through the space.

"It's just out of reach. I can't get the right angle."

Kevin seized the crowbar and began prying out the next board. This one came out more easily because the empty space next to it gave him more room to work. Once that board was out, Kevin put his hand into the gap and removed the plastic package. It was the size of a sheet of paper and wrapped in several layers.

"There's an old lantern back in the house," said

Steve, walking toward the open doors. "I'll get it. We could use more light."

Marcie held the flashlight over Kevin's shoulder as he began to take off the plastic. "Careful, it could be pretty fragile."

Kevin placed the plastic on the floor and began to slowly peel it away. Once it was completely unfolded, it revealed two pieces of paper torn from an old-fashioned child's composition book covered on both sides with handwriting. He picked up a sheet of paper; it stuck to the plastic. As he gently pulled it free, something metallic flashed in the light and rolled off the plastic. Kevin caught it just before it reached the gap in the floorboards.

"What is it?" Marcie answered.

"A ring, I think," Kevin said, handing it up to her.

It was a simple wedding ring. Marcie looked at the inside of it under the flashlight: *Felicia and Rudy 1936.*

"It's Felicia's wedding ring," Marcie said. "I guess she left it behind. I wonder why Quentin put it in with this stuff."

Kevin didn't reply. He was sitting on the floor reading the page. Marcie sat down next to him and read along.

To Whom It May Concern:

Since I don't know who you are that's reading this, I'm just going to assume that you know nothing about what happened back in 1944. I'm going to tell you the whole story, so you know the truth.

In late June of '44, Jack McDermott, the chief of police in Doric, Vermont, came to me and said that he'd like the use of my barn for a Sunday after-noon. I asked him why, and he said that it was for official business. When I asked him for details, he said that it would be better if I didn't know, and that he didn't want anyone else around on the day. He warned me that if I didn't help him, things would go hard for me. A while later we arranged the date when he'd use the barn. It would be an afternoon when my daughter-in-law, Felicia, would be in town at a church meeting, and I said that I'd take my grandson, Sel, down to the creek to do some fishing.

All that's what I did, nothing more. When Sel and I came back from the creek, we found Jake Heller, Matt Carter, and George Fuller hanging dead from a beam in the barn. I called the police, of course, and when Chief McDermott came out with a cou-ple of his men, I took him aside and asked what had happened. He pretended not to know what I was talking about. When I kept at him, he warned me that at the moment I was his prime suspect, and unless I wanted to get into a whole heap of trouble, I'd keep my mouth shut. And that's what I did.

But my daughter-in-law, Felicia, wouldn't let it go. George Fuller had been a particular friend of hers. And he had hinted to her just before he died that he might have a big surprise for her in the next few days, one that might involve the farm. I didn't know this at the time, but I found out later from McDermott that he had told the three men that I was willing to sell the farm out from under Rudy for the right price. He told them to keep quiet about it because of the feeling in town about folks cheating our men in the armed forces.

Anyway, Felicia kept at me because she knew that I hadn't much cared for George. I think that made her suspect that I'd been involved. She hated me at that time for reasons I never fully understood. After Rudy was killed, things got even worse. She came to me one day and said that I had to tell her what had happened or she'd go to the state police and tell them why I wanted to kill George. I told McDermott that he had to convince her not to do that. He arranged to come out to the farm to look over the scene of the crime again. He planned it on a day when Felicia would be alone. I don't know what happened, but when I came back, Felicia was gone. I never saw her again, but I did find her wedding ring under the dresser in her bedroom. When I went out to the barn, it looked as if somebody had taken up a lot of the floorboards and dug a hole. I nailed them back into place and never told anybody about it.

Things have been hard for Sel and me lately. The farm has been doing real poorly. I blame it on the bad luck we've had ever since those men were hanged. I think Rudy's dying like that in an accident after the war was over was God's way of punishing me for what I've done. I think McDermott owes me for all that's happened. I've talked to him about it lately, and he's promised to come over and discuss it with me. I'm writing all of this down and putting it in a safe place just in case things don't work out. I thought about telling Sel where to find this, but I don't want him to know that I was responsible for the death of his mom. He's all I have left. All I can hope is that if anything happens to me, the truth will come out someday.

Quentin Hayes

"Quite a story," Kevin said after a long moment had passed. He put the letter back into the plastic along with the ring.

Marcie nodded. "Old Quentin really whitewashed his role in things. There's no mention of his sexual harassment of Felicia or his hatred for George Fuller. And I'll bet McDermott told him exactly what he was going to do in the barn that day. Once Quentin heard that George Fuller was going to be one of the victims, I'll bet he was all for it. The thing I don't understand is why McDermott was so eager get revenge."

"That's one question I think I have the answer to," Kevin said. "Before I ran into Dad, I was doing some research at the *Courier.* Joe Campbell's sister told me about McDermott's visit to her home. He said something to her about how sad it was to lose a brother. That got me thinking, so I checked through the obituaries for the early forties. Jack had a much younger brother who was killed in combat just two months before the three men were hanged."

"So Jack McDermott, like everybody else in town, knew about what those guys had done, then his brother gets killed, and suddenly he feels that justice has to be served. He decides that these drunks and thieves who hurt servicemen and their families should be punished, even if it meant going outside the law."

"I know that sounds kind of crazy."

"Stranger things have happened."

"I suppose. But I checked, and Jack has been dead since the sixties. That means somebody else killed Sel."

"Somebody who had a lot to lose if this story came out."

A match flared in the darkness, and a moment later the barn was illuminated by the warm glow of an oil lamp.

"I brought us some light," Steve said.

When he saw the letter in Kevin's hand, he sighed. Then he reached behind his back, and a gun appeared in his hand.

"Why don't you both stand up?" Steve said, gesturing sharply with the gun.

As they got to their feet, Marcie picked up the crowbar that was on the floor beside her, hoping that McDermott wouldn't notice. She held it behind her back as she scrambled to her feet.

"I see you've found what I was looking for," Steve said, looking at the paper in Kevin's hand. "I searched the house for that. I even went under the eaves of the attic and sorted through that box the same way the two of you did."

"You knew we did that?" Kevin asked.

"Of course. I put everything back in a certain order after I searched the house the evening of Sel's death."

"*Murder,* you mean," Marcie said.

Steve shrugged. "I never expected the papers would be that hard to find. Sel didn't impress me as being very imaginative. Unfortunately, by the time I realized that I couldn't find the papers, he was already unconscious, and I couldn't wake him up to question him further. I had other plans for Sel. Since I was the executor of his will, I didn't figure that would be any problem. Once he was dead, I'd be free to search the property to my heart's content."

"How did you end up as his executor?" Kevin asked.

"Just lucky. My father and uncle had always been nice to him, so when he wanted to make a will, I was his first choice."

"And after he found the letter, Sel came around demanding money?" Kevin asked.

"Of course. He planned to pick up where his grandfather left off. He gave me a brief summary of what Quentin had written, then he suggested that we have the kind of arrangement like the one his grandfather had wanted to have with my great-grandfather. I don't think it ever occurred to Sel that my Granddad Jack had murdered his grandfather. Perhaps if it had, he would have thought twice about blackmailing me. He might have suspected that murder was in the blood."

"You *knew* that your great-grandfather had killed Quentin Hayes?" Marcie asked.

"Not knew, exactly. But I'd heard lots of family stories about my great-grandfather. He had something of a reputation as being a law unto himself. When Sel told me what Quentin had planned to do, I figured right away that his fall down the stairs was no accident."

"And did you know that he hanged those men in the barn because of the death of his brother?" Kevin asked.

A puzzled expression came over Steve's face. "That

had nothing to do with it. Not directly, anyway. When Jack's younger brother died, he swore that his son, my Grandfather Luke, would never go to war. He sent him to Boston to study so no one would notice he wasn't serving; then he blackmailed a clerk for the local draft board who'd gotten into some legal trouble into losing his son's paperwork."

"So what went wrong?" Marcie asked.

"George Fuller went to Boston on some bank business, and he saw Luke on the street. They'd been old friends during grade school. They went out and had quite a few drinks. Luke got mellow and figured that he was safe telling an old friend who also wasn't in the military what had happened."

"And George came back, told his two friends, and they decided to blackmail your great-grandfather," Marcie said.

"I assume so. But I don't know for certain. When Luke sobered up and realized what he had done, he confessed to his father. Jack told him not to worry about it. That if there were any problems, he'd take care of it. I can only suppose that they approached him with a blackmail threat, but he never told Luke."

"And after the war was over, your grandfather came back to town?" asked Kevin.

"With a vague story of having worked in Washington for some special agency during the war. He made it sound very hush-hush. No one asked many questions. They probably figured that he'd been in intelligence. Luke told my father the story about dodging the draft just in case it ever came back to haunt the practice, and my father told me. But neither one of them connected it with the hanging men because Jack never told them what he'd had to do to keep the family secret. I never suspected either, until Sel came to me with his blackmail demand."

"Your grandfather must have had his suspicions."

Steve shrugged. "My grandfather was a fine man and a good lawyer. But can you blame him if he never inquired too closely into what his father had done to protect him? In his place, would you have really wanted to know?"

"So four men tried to blackmail Jack, if you include Quentin, and he killed them all," said Marcie.

Steve nodded. "You can't really blame him. They brought it on themselves."

"And Felicia Hayes?" Marcie asked.

"I'd like to think that was one act even Jack was truly ashamed of doing." Steve paused, his face gaunt. "But once you start down that road, it's hard to stop. I know that now."

"But why did you murder Sel?" Kevin asked. "Nothing he said would have reflected badly on you. The voters in Vermont are a pretty open-minded bunch. They wouldn't have blamed you for what your great-grandfather did. They'd have kept reelecting to state office you as long as you did a decent job."

Steve McDermott gave a bitter laugh. "Do you think I want to stay in Montpelier for the rest of my life? And if I ever wanted to run for national office like the House or Senate, this would be hung around my neck like an albatross. The story of the hanging men isn't just about a triple homicide. It's a local legend. And folks like the two of you would make certain that the story got wide coverage. Every time I got up to speak, people would be thinking that there stood the great-grandson of a serial killer. I couldn't let that little nothing of a man do that to me. Maybe he would have drunk himself to death in a few years, but he liked to talk, and I was sure that sooner or later he'd slip up and give away the truth."

"So you killed him and tried to make it look like a suicide," said Marcie.

"I couldn't do a perfect job of it, but I figured that Roylston wasn't going to look into it any more than he had to. And I was right. This would have been old news by now if not for the two of you."

"That's why you tried to scare me off by putting that note on the desk at the inn."

"Guilty as charged. That noose hanging over your head was also my doing. I put it out here the night before you were due to come out to search the farm. I thought it might scare you off."

"And is that why you suggested to me that I really might be sensing ghostly vibrations in the barn?" Marcie asked.

McDermott nodded and gave Marcie a sad smile. "Please believe me, I never wanted it to come to this."

"And is that why you were nice to me?" Marcie asked. "As a way of avoiding suspicion?"

"That was only part of it," Steve said. "But none of that matters now."

McDermott swung the gun toward Kevin. "Now why don't you come over here and put what you found down on the floor right in front of me? Once I have it, the two of you can go. It will be just your word against mine."

Kevin glanced at Marcie. She shook her head.

"This story isn't worth dying over," McDermott said.

"I don't believe you're going to let us go no matter what we do," Marcie said.

"Why not?" Steve asked.

"I don't think you're willing to take the chance that no one will listen to us," said Marcie. "Once you have the evidence, I think we're dead."

"You could easily be dead anyway. I can shoot both of you and take Quentin's letter. No one will hear anything this far out of town."

"But then you'll have to dispose of two bodies and two vehicles. That won't be easy," said Marcie.

"And my father knows what I'm working on. You know enough about him to realize that he won't give up until he's got some answers. I'm sure Marcie's boss will be the same."

Marcie nodded vigorously.

"Then I guess I'll have to give people a different version of the events." He picked the lamp up from the floor and swung it in his hand for a moment. "This is an old oil lamp I found in the barn just the other day. I put a new wick in it and was surprised to see that it still worked just fine. But these old lamps aren't nearly as safe as the new ones. I'll bet if I just tipped it over, the burning oil would turn an old barn like this into an inferno in no time. People would think that the two of you were trespassing, doing some amateur investigating of your own, and happened to knock over the lamp. A tragic accident."

"Won't work," Marcie said quickly. "As soon as that lamp goes over, we'll run for the door, so you'll have to shoot us anyway. We're not going to make it easy for you."

Steve McDermott stood for a moment looking into space. The fact that he was calmly examining scenarios frightened Marcie because she figured he was bright enough to come up with one that would work.

"The two of you came out here to search," Steve said slowly, "but it turns out that Kevin had more on his mind than buried treasure. He got violent when you wouldn't go along with his demands and knocked you out. Then he was afraid of what you might do when you regained consciousness, so he decided to stage another hanging to deflect suspicion from himself. I came into the yard right about then and saw your cars. I got into the barn just in time to see him hang you from the beam. I shot him, but, sadly, it was too late."

"A pretty elaborate story," Marcie said, trying to sound scornful, even though her mouth was dry. It was really a pretty good plan.

"I think it will work," McDermott said. "So I guess the first thing I have to do now is to shoot you," he said, turning toward Kevin.

Marcie had been holding the crowbar so long that her grip had stiffened, and sweat made the metal slippery in her hand. Steve was fifteen feet away, a long throw of the heavy bar. She would aim for the center of his body and throw with all her might, hoping to hit something. Even if she missed, it would distract him.

"Toss the letter and ring onto the ground when I say three," she whispered quickly to Kevin. "Then you go to the right, and I'll go to the left." She had no idea if Kevin understood what she was saying, but there wasn't time to find out.

As Steve began to raise the gun to fire, Marcie shouted, "Three!"

Out of the corner of her eye she saw the letter hit the floor of the barn, distracting Steve. She immediately threw the crowbar with a sweeping forward motion of her arm. It flew end over end and hit McDermott solidly in the arm holding the lamp. She heard a gasp of pain followed by the shattering of glass. But by then Marcie was running to the left, hoping to get behind McDermott and out the door. The sound of gunfire deafened her as she ran toward the open doorway.

When Marcie got to the door, she turned back to look for Kevin. Flames were leaping up from a bale of hay near where the lamp must have fallen; they quickly jumped from bale to bale across the barn. By their light she could see McDermott searching the floor for the letter that Kevin had dropped. She looked to her left, wondering where Kevin was. Had that shot she heard hit him? It would only be a matter of seconds before McDermott found the letter, and then he would be coming after them.

Finally she saw Kevin running toward her, trying to stay in the shadows. She glanced back at McDermott. He had the letter in his hand and was turning toward the door. He'd have a clear shot at both of them in the doorway. She squatted down to make herself a smaller target.

"Hurry, Kevin!" she shouted.

A gust of wind blew through the walls of the barn, making a sound like voices talking just beyond the range of human hearing. The flames suddenly rose up, reaching the rafters. As Marcie watched, smoke swept across the roofline as if it had a mind of its own.

Kevin gave up on concealment and broke directly for the door, but McDermott saw him, raised the gun, and took a step forward. Suddenly he stumbled and pitched forward. An instant later he was up on one knee, trying to free his foot from the hole in the floor as the flames quickly spread across the dry barn. McDermott glanced up in desperation as he heard the wooden rafters above his head snapping from the heat of the fire.

"What's happening?" Kevin asked, kneeling next to Marcie.

"I think Steve caught his foot in the gap we made in the floorboards."

McDermott saw them in the doorway. "Help me!" he called out.

"Throw the gun over here, and we'll come and help you," Marcie replied.

He paused for a moment as if considering the idea; then he returned to trying to free his foot.

"We should get out of here," Kevin said. "If he does free himself, he'll be able to shoot us before we can get away."

"We can't just leave him here to die in the fire. He's going to have to give up soon."

"Throw out the gun, and we'll help you!" Marcie shouted again.

The cloud of smoke descended over Steve, and he disappeared from view. All she heard was coughing. She called out to McDermott one more time, but her words were drowned out by a roaring sound as a hole opened in the roof of the barn. Flames shot upward as if reaching for the sky, and there was a burst of heat and flame that forced Marcie and Kevin out the door. A second later Marcie risked a glance back inside.

"No!" she heard Steve roar.

He was standing upright, waving his arms like a man fighting off a swarm of bees as he tried to push away the smoke engulfing him. He screamed and with a convulsive movement pulled his foot free of the floor. But by then the smoke had gathered around to the burning beam above his head. The beam slowly bent and gave way with a crack like a rifle shot. As it came down, it appeared to Marcie as if the noose that was hanging there swung down over Steve's head. Then the beam slammed into him, and he disappeared into the fire.

Chapter Nineteen

Marcie pulled into the parking lot of *Roaming New England Magazine* and sat behind the wheel for a moment, looking across the wetlands to the ocean. She had unexpectedly spent last night at the Doric Inn. By the time she and Kevin had gotten done telling their story to the police, it was too late for her to travel to her motel, and although she was thoroughly sick of Doric, she was too exhausted to go anywhere else. That morning she had gotten up early and left before breakfast, eager to be gone.

She had called Amanda at home after midnight and given her a brief account of what had happened. Amanda had said that she definitely shouldn't travel until the next day and then she should return directly to the office. Marcie had said that she was fine and could continue with her planned trip. However, Amanda had insisted that they should reschedule the interviews for the next week. Marcie kept asking her over and over again whether she thought there was a story in all this that the magazine could use. Amanda had reassured her that with an ending like Steve McDermott's death in the barn, they'd certainly find some way to fit it into the "Weird Happenings" column.

As she sat in the car, the memories replayed themselves once again in her head, as had been happening all night. The police and firemen arriving almost simultaneously after Kevin's phone call. The barn already completely in flames, beyond any saving.

Chief Roylston had allowed them to drive their own vehicles to the police station, but only under his personal escort. Marcie suspected that their interrogation would have been far rougher if Kevin's father hadn't shown up soon after. Looking shaken by what had almost happened to his son, he had demanded that they be allowed to make their statements and leave without delay. Roylston had quickly agreed, perhaps hoping that the sooner all of this was dealt with, the less likely it was that it would become a major news event.

Marcie didn't think he was going to be that lucky. Kevin's father seemed to have undergone a conversion and was now looking at this story as an opportunity to expose a notorious old crime. Even though Quentin Hayes' letter had been destroyed in the blaze, Mr. Murray promised Kevin that they'd find a way to run the story. He figured that when McDermott's body was found in the ashes with a gun, it would go a long way toward corroborating their version of events. After briefly introducing Marcie, Kevin had moved with his father to the other end of the hallway for a private conversation.

As Marcie had sat on the hard wooden bench waiting for the police to say she could leave, her tired mind began to drift. She hoped that Felicia's wedding ring would also be found in the ashes. Maybe it could be arranged to have it given to her friend, Ellen Barkum, the one person alive who still cared about her.

When she was gently shaken by the shoulder, Marcie looked up, startled, and saw Kevin standing over her.

"Sorry to disturb you."

"I guess I fell asleep. Can we go yet?" she asked.

Kevin nodded. "The police just gave us permission. Would you like me to follow you to the inn?

"No, I'll be fine."

"I've just had a long talk with my father. We've decided that it's time that I come on board full-time at the *Courier*. This story should prove that I have what it takes to be a real reporter."

"That was true from the beginning. I could see it when we first began to work together."

"Thank you," Kevin said softly. He gave her a long look. "I suppose there's no chance that we could get together again."

Marcie smiled. "I'm sure we'll run into each other, since we're both covering the same turf. It's great to have a friend in the profession."

She put out her hand, and after a moment a sad-looking but resigned Kevin took it in his. "You know that I'm not like Steve McDermott. I really do like you."

Marcie gave him a tearful smile. "And that means a lot to me."

Marcie forced her mind back to the present. She got out of the car, slung her laptop over her shoulder, and headed toward the back door. Before she was halfway there, Amanda came out and walked toward her. She looked as professional as ever in a cream blouse, straight black skirt, and a tasteful gold necklace. Only her precarious high heels showed that she had a wilder side. Her face was grave. Marcie knew that she must be upset over the late-night call, and probably even more disturbed over the bungled trip. Rescheduling all those interviews was bound to be a nightmare.

"I'm sorry," Marcie began as Amanda drew closer.

Before she could say more, Amanda broke into an awkward run and threw her arms around Marcie. "I'm so glad that you're all right."

"I'm fine," Marcie managed to say as her throat tightened. They clung to each other for a moment, neither one able to speak.

"I guess you got a real sense of history on this trip," Amanda said, as she pushed back her hair, which allowed her to surreptitiously brush away a tear.

"It's certainly different when you get it from the source rather than from a book."

"And you hinted that there might have been some supernatural experiences?" Amanda asked.

"Hard to know. I'll tell you about it later," Marcie said.

Marcie frowned and studied the ground as they started walking back toward the building.

"Experiencing this weird stuff can get to you. It did to me," Amanda said. "Your entire sense of reality tilts."

"That's not what's bothering me."

"What, then?"

Marcie shrugged. "You always hear about World War II as being this great, noble thing, and in a lot of ways I guess it was. But not everyone was a hero."

"You mean those men who were hanged."

"Yeah. But I'm also thinking about the people in Doric who didn't seem to care about justice. They didn't want to look into what had happened to the hanging men because they figured they got what they deserved—even if it was murder. They were willing to forget about the law in order to get revenge. And they—the whole town—got away with it."

Amanda reached out and squeezed Marcie's arm.

"You mean they got away with it up until now. Your story will force them to admit to what they did. Even if most of the people responsible are dead, the town won't be able to hide what happened any longer." Amanda paused for a moment. "The most we can do as journalists is make people face up to the truth."

Marcie smiled at her friend. "You're right. And I guess sometimes that's doing quite a lot."